Awakening Passion

Sexy Stories Collection

VOLUME 20

5 EROTIC SHORT STORIES

JESSICA BANKMAN

Publisher's Note: This is a work of fiction. Names,
characters, places, and incidents are a product of
the author's imagination. Locales and public
names are sometimes used for atmospheric
purposes. Any resemblance to actual people, living
or dead, or to businesses, companies, events,
institutions, or locales is completely coincidental.

Awakening Passion/ Jessica Bankman. -- 1st ed.
Xplicit Press, an imprint of TLM Media LLC

ISBN-13: 978-1-62327-551-8
ISBN-10: 1-62327-551-2
eISBN: 978-1-62327-601-0

Printed in the United States of America

CONTENTS

1 A DANGEROUS NIGHT

Heading home was one of the best things Sarah could do for herself. She sighed in relief, grabbing her new romance novel out of her carry-on and melting into the back of her seat. Spending the last two weeks with Tim Schtick was almost more than she could handle. His cockiness drove her up the wall; his loud, thunderous voice was still ringing in her ears.

"God, who thought spending four years in liberal arts school, would guarantee a career like this one..." Sarah thought to herself.

All of Sarah's life, she dreamed of becoming a journalist. When other girls her age growing up wanted to become models, actresses, or even princesses, Sarah knew that she wanted to report, to write, and to maybe even be in the limelight a little. A beautiful news reporter that men would swoon over or a top notch writer for Time Magazine; something of that sort, something fabulous, something fun, something exciting. Sarah worked hard throughout her schooling in order to get top grades. She didn't want to have to struggle to get accepted anywhere. She wanted her choice schools to want her; and they did. When she got accepted to her dream college, she worked even harder, graduating top of her class with a 4.0 GPA. When her career counselor told her upon graduation that The Travel Connection was interested in her, Sarah thought she finally made it, that all of her hard work had finally paid off.

Little did Sarah know she wasn't going to be in the spotlight. Hell, she wasn't going to be reporting anything, period. What Sarah was going to do was research. Research exotic locations and send other, more beautiful, women on the trip. Not only was Sarah's job lacking glamour, she wasn't the icon of beauty, either. She was average, plain, and normal looking.

Sarah's childhood dream of being the beautiful news reporter was turned upside down when she realized upon entering high school what competition really meant. Her body was late to enter puberty, and even when it did, it didn't shell out the gifts of large breasts, or large anything for that matter. When her breasts grew to a B-cup, Sarah prayed to God that they'd jump up one more size, but they never did. She never grew too tall either; she was rather petite, making her ability to compete with the tall model-esque girls in her class tough. Not to mention it was impossible to find a pair of jeans that fit right.

So here was Sarah, stuck in a dull career and a dull figure. Rather than feel helpless, she embraced her destiny and kept going. She wasn't going to beat herself up over it and she wasn't going to try to fight it, and with the salary she was making at The Travel Connection, she really couldn't complain. Even it meant having a boring job and putting up with Tim Schtick for the rest of her life.

The romance novel was starting to get hot and Sarah was beginning to feel uncomfortable. She hadn't been touched by a man in so long that she almost completely forgot how good it felt to be turned on. Maybe it was weird that she was turned on by a book written by some author who created fake characters, but Sarah didn't care. The characters were sexy and the sex scenes so steamy that although Sarah knew she couldn't relieve herself now on the plane while sitting next to some teenager, she made a mental note to schedule in some alone time once she reached her hometown of Buffalo, NY. Sarah decided to put the book down for now; she wasn't going to allow herself to be all hot and bothered and have no way to deal with it. She figured she'd spend the last hour of her flight napping. She needed some rest anyhow. Sarah started to put her book away, but all of a sudden, she heard Tim's ringtone chiming out from her cell phone. Damnit, so much for relaxation.

"Hello?" Sarah answered, gritting through her teeth.

"Sarah, baby! How's my best girl?" responded Tim, sugaring her up with his

California accent.

"Well, Tim..." Sarah said annoyed, ignoring his pretend charm. "I'm on a plane, heading home right now. I'm done with the project as was agreed and I'm getting ready to relax in Buffalo for the next two weeks. What can I help you with today, boss?"

"Gee, Sarah, way to sound excited to talk to the man who's giving you a very new, exciting position," Tim said. "Do me a favor when you reach Buffalo and buy a ticket to Zanzibar for the next morning. You're going to be our new Romantic Destinations host!"

"What?" exclaimed Sarah, trying to tone down the excitement in her voice. "You mean I'm finally going to get to host something? I'm finally going to get my first big break?"

"Yes, you are doll face! You're our new Romantic Destinations host!" exclaimed Tim, repeating himself.

"Wait..." questioned Sarah. "What happened to Dee Dee? Romantic Destinations was her show for years. I mean Romantic Destinations is Dee Dee Valentine! Without her, there's no show!"

"Dee Dee decided to call it quits today. She's headed in a new direction. Posing for Playboy or something," Tim said, laughing nervously. "But never mind that! I took it upon myself to make sure you're our new Romantic Destinations girl, since you're so hardworking and all."

"Oh, really?" replied Sarah, who knew there was something more to it than what Tim was telling her. "Why did she quit, Tim? Let's get this straight, stop lying to me."

Tim sighed on the other end. "We couldn't afford her anymore, Sarah. She's refused to renew her contract now for weeks and when I finally asked her about it today, she simply wanted too much money. She's been offered so many other contracts now by companies that could buy and sell us any day of the week. We just couldn't afford her."

Tim paused. "But there's one more thing Sarah. You have to dress sexy. You have to sell sex on Romantic Destinations. You just do. That's what Dee Dee did and that's why we're still on air. Hell, that's why Dee Dee has done so well for herself. So wear a bikini any chance you get and try to flirt. I mean, if you know how."

"So what are you telling me? That you want me to take this position on the salary that I am making now? And you want me to do it half-naked? You know, I think I like researching, Tim. I'll just stick with that," said Sarah angrily.

"Sarah, please!" Tim begged. "What about $90,000 added to your salary this year, and we'll sort through the rest of the details once you get back to LA?"

"I'm in," said Sarah, hiding her enthusiasm. "I'll call you tomorrow, before I take flight to Zanzibar."

"Thank you, thank you!" shouted Tim joyously. "I promise you, Sarah, you won't regret this. Just remember to show off your body a little and this might change your life forever."

"Perhaps," replied Sarah. "Perhaps you just may be right. For once."

The island exceeded Sarah's expectations. She spent her whole life researching exotic locations like this, but never had the opportunity to visit one. Maybe Tim was right. Maybe this whole experience would change her life forever. Either way, Sarah felt like for once in her life she was ready to shine. Even if it meant roaming the island half-naked.

Walking up to her hotel, Sarah saw the most gorgeous man that she had ever laid eyes on. He was standing in front of the entrance, smoking a cigar. As much as Sarah despised the smoke of cigars, she didn't mind the smell of it as long as it was coming from this man. He looked as exotic as the island itself, but Sarah knew he wasn't a local. Russian, Romanian, somewhere around that part of the world, perhaps. Whatever he was, he was a bottle of tall, dark, and handsome that Sarah wanted to drink right up. His eyes were his most striking feature; something about them so dark and mysterious, and Sarah wasn't thinking about his eye color.

Sarah took a deep breath and walked towards the entrance, almost coming face to face with the man. The man put his cigar out and to Sarah's surprise, started to speak.

"Excuse me, Miss," he said in a thick Russian accent. "Let me get those bags for you. They look too heavy for a woman of your structure to carry."

Sarah felt her cheeks start to grow warmer

than they already were. Russian, she thought to herself. He's definitely Russian.

"Why, thank you. You're so kind," she replied.

The man took her bags from her and held the door open. Once he entered the lobby, he placed them on a cart and told the bellboy to bring them to her room. He then tipped him $50 and excused himself, shining his big, flashing smile as he said goodbye to Sarah.

"Goodbye, and thank you," Sarah said, thinking to herself that she hoped to see this man again during her island stay.

The rest of the day Sarah didn't think about the handsome man who took her luggage. She focused on her work, enjoying every minute of it. Sarah always knew that she wanted to do something like this, but never knew she'd be such a natural at it. Even her cameraman made a comment about how well she was doing connecting with the locals and making Zanzibar seem so interesting. It wasn't hard for Sarah, because she truly did enjoy the place so far. The people were friendly, with such a rich and diverse culture. The beaches were breathtaking, crowded with interesting locals and tourists alike. And the food was to die for. Being a seafood lover and having the experience to try dishes made with fresh lobster and crab was enough for Sarah to declare Zanzibar one of the best destinations in the world. Sarah even surprised herself at how calm she was wearing the tiniest bikini that she'd ever seen. She felt glamorous, beautiful, and confident; her cheeks didn't even flush when a man turned to get a second look at her. She really was starting to enjoy this new role and easily fell into character.

Hours had passed and the sun was starting to set when Sarah and her crew finally decided to call it quits for the night. Sarah was full of so much life and energy all day that she never realized how much exertion she had put on her body. Her body was spent, her feet ached and her back felt tight. She thought about heading to her room for the night and calling it a day, but the idea of just lying in bed seemed so boring now. Anyways, if she tried to fall asleep right now, she probably couldn't. Her mind was still buzzing and she was full of so much energy.

Instead, she'd thought she'd head down to the hotel's bar for a while and have a few drinks. Drinking always made her relaxed and tired; it was one of her favorite ways to unwind. Besides, she could get to know more about the tourists and locals at the bar. People tended to talk more freely and really open up when they were slightly intoxicated.

On her way to the bar, Sarah could hear local music blasting on the speakers and different voices chattering and laughing. She entered a luxurious room that obviously had been designed for tourists. Palm trees, local flowers, drinks lined with little umbrellas. The floor was covered with sand, and the bar had sand sprinkled across it. There was a large pool in the corner of the bar, where hotel guests were drunkenly swimming. Everyone looked like they were having the time of their lives and Sarah wanted to be a part of it.

"Sex on the Beach," requested Sarah to the bartender teasingly.

"Ooooh...a popular drink," the bartender replied with a smile in his eyes, heading to create the concoction.

Sarah tipped him when he returned with her drink and started sipping, settling into her chair, taking in the bar's ambience. It felt so good to relax. It felt so good to be there. It felt so good to finally fulfill her dreams and be an on-film reporter. She watched as groups of people laughed and couples flirted openly. She heard screams from the pool as a woman was splashed by two playful bachelors. She examined the art, the people, the culture, just taking it all in one breath at a time.

What Sarah didn't see was the man in the back of the bar who was closely watching her. The man who was yearning for her, looking at her lips as she slowly sipped her drink. Those lips, he thought to himself, would look good on something else, something a little more delicious than a fruity drink.

"Is this seat taken?" echoed a familiar voice behind Sarah.

His voice startled Sarah out of her daze and she turned around to see the man who had carried her luggage into the hotel pointing at the empty chair beside her. She almost couldn't catch her breath; he was so damn good looking.

"This chair?" questioned Sarah. "No, it isn't."

"Hi," said the man, as he settled into the empty seat. "My name is Nikolai. Nikolai Petroff. It's a pleasure to meet you. Well, to meet you again."

Sarah laughed, her eyes sparkling. "Hi, my name's Sarah Whiteman, and the pleasure is all mine."

Sarah was on her fourth or fifth Sex on The Beach when she realized she had lost count. She was looking into Nikolai's big, beautiful, brown eyes. Two hours had passed and Sarah still wasn't feeling tired. If anything, she felt more alive than ever. Nikolai was charming and funny, making Sarah laugh the night away. He said very little about himself, but Sarah didn't mind that. This wasn't a date anyway. They were just two strangers in a bar conversing. Sarah was happy to tell Nikolai about herself, she wanted to make a good impression. She didn't want to make this hot piece of Russian man think she was just some dumb American girl. She wanted him to like her for her.

Nikolai was attracted to Sarah for her intelligence, but he was becoming increasingly attracted to luscious her body. He could see her nipples hardening underneath her white tank top and couldn't help but feel his manhood become rock solid underneath his pants. He was hungry for this woman's flesh, and wanted to take her to her room and ravish her body.

"Sarah, I don't mean to be so forward," said Nikolai, hesitating. "But ever since I met you earlier..."

Sarah stopped his words, placing her index finger on his lips as she leaned in to kiss him. This moment was almost too good to be true and she didn't want to talk about it. She just wanted to experience it. Nikolai responded, accepting her kiss, licking her lower lip.

"I want you," said Sarah as she backed out of the kiss. "My room, now."

Nikolai gulped down the last of his drink and grabbed Sarah by the hand. The two walked toward the elevator; once inside, they began kissing and ravishing each other's bodies. Nikolai, with his strong, muscular upper body, picked Sarah up and held her to his waist, pressing his cock against the outline of her pussy. They licked and mouth-fucked each other's tongues until they were abruptly interrupted by the ding of the elevator reaching its landing. Sarah jumped onto Nikolai's back and rode him as a stallion until they reached her hotel door, laughing and giggling the whole way there. Nikolai bent over and let Sarah down as she fumbled with her key trying to open the hotel door. Once the hotel door opened, Nikolai picked up Sarah again, this time throwing her onto the bed.

"I want you, woman," said Nikolai. "I want you like I've never wanted any other woman before."

Nikolai leaned over Sarah on the bed and kissed her passionately, taking full control of the situation. He drew figure eights up her arms, encircling her, until he reached her chest. He grabbed her perky tit, making Sarah moan out in pleasure, while pushing his tongue into her mouth. She began feverishly sucking his tongue, tugging on his lips. Nikolai pulled down her tank top strap, revealing her perky breast. He placed his tongue onto its soft skin, licking her nipple. Nikolai was driving Sarah wild; she felt her pussy start to soak in its own juices. She couldn't wait for him to place his fingers inside of it, toying with her until she felt like she'd explode.

Nikolai must've read her mind. He went from licking her nipple to full on sucking it, placing one hand to ravish her other tit, and his other hand unzipping her jeans. Sarah wanted him to touch her pussy now; she quickly unzipped her jeans and threw them off of the bed. She tore off her silky blue panties, throwing them on top of her jeans. Nikolai felt the perfectly trimmed fur on top of her mound, which turned him on even more. He liked a well-trimmed bush and wasn't a fan of shaved pussy. Hers was exactly the kind that he liked.

Still sucking her left tit and playing with her right one, Nikolai took his left hand and unfolded the sides of her vagina. He used his fingers to torture her clit at first and then stuck one, then two, fingers into her hot, slippery hole. Sarah was wetter than he expected and the thought that drove him wild. Her moans were so loud and sexy, Nikolai wanted to make them even louder. He pumped his fingers in and out of her velvety pussy harder and faster. Nikolai was good at making

Sarah wet; she almost felt like she was going to cum. She wanted to save her release for Nikolai's cock, so she decided that she'd change it up a bit.

"Take off your pants," Sarah demanded. "I want to see that cock of yours."

Nikolai pulled his fingers out of Sarah's wet pussy and licked her nipple one last time. He stood up, removed his shirt, and slowly started unbuckling his pants, teasing Sarah. He stood for a second in his boxer briefs, letting Sarah admire his package. He was big. Once he took off his underwear, Sarah thought he was the most well-hung man that she had ever had the pleasure to fuck. Nikolai leaned his perfectly sculpted nine-inch cock towards Sarah, who was lubing her hand with spit in order to properly give the man a hand job. She used both hands to bounce up and down on Nikolai's cock, her pussy dripping in anticipation for it to be inside of her.

"Let me taste it," Sarah requested.

Nikolai's cock sprang forward as Sarah put her rosy red lips on top of it. She suctioned her lips around it and sucked up and down, bobbing her head. He tasted so good, she thought as she pulled off of his dick, teasing the head with her lips.

"God, you almost made me cum," said Nikolai. "I'm going to fuck that wet cunt of yours, you deserve it."

Nikolai pinned Sarah to the bed by her wrists and got on top of her, placing his throbbing cock into her slick hole. Sarah had the tightest pussy he had ever had before and he was going to treat it well tonight. He throbbed up and down, fucking her slowly at first, but increasing his speed until he was fucking her so hard he was hitting her back wall. Sarah was screaming, the pain felt so good, she just wanted to cum all over his big, fat, Russian dick.

"Not yet, baby," Nikolai whispered. "You've been such a bad girl tonight; I want to get you doggy-style. Turn around."

Sarah was almost at her climax, but the idea of this Russian man ramming his dick into her pussy behind her was worth the wait. She turned around and put her knees and elbows on the bed, already fingering her pussy before he shoved his fat dick inside of her. This made Nikolai excited and his dick shot pearls of pre-cum before he stuffed it back into her. He slapped her ass and rode behind her slow and hard. Sarah was screaming louder and louder. He wanted to feel her drizzle down onto his hard cock.

"Cum for me baby," he said, grabbing her tit with his right hand.

Sarah's release came like thunder as she roared into the island night, her white milk creaming onto his dick as she vibrated up and down releasing it. Nikolai, seeing her cum covering his dick, felt himself rupture. He didn't want to cum inside of Sarah's pussy, so he pulled out and shot his load all over her beautiful ass.

Leaving Sarah withered on the bed; he walked towards the bathroom and grabbed a towel. He came back to the bed and lovingly wiped his cum off of Sarah's ass and his still rock-hard member. He threw the towel to the floor and curled up next to Sarah's naked body. They laid in silence, Sarah quickly falling asleep to the sound of birds chirping in the morning's sunrise.

Sarah awoke to the sound of her alarm going off. She reached her arm across the bed, expecting to wrap it around Nikolai. Shock ran through Sarah's half-waken body when she realized no one was there. Maybe he was in the bathroom or on the balcony, she quickly thought to herself. She opened her eyes and saw no one in the room. Her head was spinning.

She was in disbelief, thinking maybe she dreamed the whole thing up, but when she ran her arms across her naked body and opened the folds of her still-moist vagina, Sarah knew that last night definitely had happened. She grabbed the white robe sitting on the chair next to the bed and slowly put it on. She got up, hoping to see Nikolai outside. When Sarah opened the French doors that led to the balcony, she found herself standing outside alone. She knew that Nikolai was gone. Nikolai had fucked her and left, and for the first time in her life, Sarah felt like a slut.

"I never bring men to bed after first meeting them." Sarah said to herself out loud. "What am I? Stupid? An idiot? Someone who likes to be used? What was I thinking last night? That I was just going to have sex with this man and make him mine, forever? Sarah Whiteman, you know better than that."

A tear fell from Sarah's eyes as she walked back into the room, trying to assure herself that she was going to be okay. She looked at the clock and realized that she had two hours before she and the crew would start filming.

"Well, I better get over this, and get ready," thought Sarah. "No point making a complete disaster of the entire trip."

Sarah spent another day filming, not thinking about Nikolai. This time it wasn't because she was too busy with her work, but because she didn't want to ever think of the man again. She didn't want to remember a man who saw her only as a body and nothing else, and she made a promise to herself that she would finish this job giving it her all, not filling her head with melancholy.

Sarah and her crew were making their way to the scuba diving area of the resort when they heard loud booms roar across the land. People were shouting in a foreign tongue and she could hear the screams of people on the beach. The shouts weren't those of excitement or happiness, but of fear. The screams themselves were so full of fear that they made Sarah feel afraid herself. It seemed like time had come to an abrupt stop and Sarah just stood still, unable to move. When a group of guerillas came up to Sarah and her crew, yelling orders, her cameraman had to take her hand and escort her back to the hotel. Sarah simply couldn't move.

Sarah sat in her hotel room for what seemed like hours, shaking. Each member of her crew was instructed by the hotel manager to go to his or her separate rooms. So Sarah sat in hers, alone, scared for her life.

"Yeah, this might change my life forever," Sarah muttered, mocking Tim. "It might change my life so much that I end up dead."

As the daylight dimmed and night began to set, Sarah felt herself start to come to. She wasn't shaking anymore; she was going through the motions a person goes through when they are facing the end of their life. She thought of her family, her friends, her career. She thought of the last few days that she had spent on this island, and she thought of Nikolai.

"If he cared anything about me, he might've stayed," she thought. "And maybe he might've been here to save me."

Just then, a loud knock sounded at Sarah's door. Before she could even answer it, a group of guerillas knocked it down, breaking the door off of its frame. Sarah jumped out of her chair, shrieking sounds that only a banshee could make. One of the men grabbed her, lifting her small frame off the floor with just one of his hands. He started yelling at her in a language she didn't understand and once finished, dropped her to the ground. He shook his head in frustration and then handed her a note. The man and his entourage left the room, almost as if they were never there. Sarah panicked, crumbling over onto the floor crying, the note still in her hand.

"Why is this happening to me? What do these men want on this island?"

Tim's voice echoed inside of Sarah's head, "You won't regret this..."

Time passed and Sarah finally sat up, wiping the streams of tears from her cheeks. She sighed in relief, knowing that the men had been gone for some time now. The hotel was completely silent. Sarah got ready to stand up, but stopped when she saw the crumpled mass in her hands. The note, she had completely forgot that the man handed her a note. She unfolded the tear-stained pages and began to read it:

Please do not worry. I know that you must be very afraid for your life right now, but you mustn't worry. These men mean no ill harm towards you, or any of the other tourists at this hotel. You must trust that everything will be okay. Please pack your bags. You will be escorted off this island first thing in the morning.

Even though Sarah barely slept a wink the night before, she sprang out of bed to answer the knock on the remains of her door. She knew that knock was regarding her safety. That knock meant Sarah's life. She may have loved the island and its charm at the beginning of her trip, but it had quickly turned into a dark, hellish place that she couldn't wait to get away from. She grabbed the robe off of the chair and hurried to answer it.

"Good morning, ma'am," curtsied a young male hotel attendant. His accent was thick; Sarah knew he was a local. "Your boat is parked at the port. I have orders that you must dress and board the boat within the next fifteen minutes. It's too dangerous to waste time."

"Yes... Yes..." Sarah stammered. "I'll quickly get ready and grab my things."

The young man kindly excused himself and Sarah rushed to her dresser, tossing everything into her suitcases. She didn't have time to think, nor did she care to at this point. A thought crossed her mind that maybe she shouldn't so eagerly trust this boat ride that she knew nothing about, but in a time of such desperate measures, Sarah knew now wasn't the time to make choices. She headed to the bathroom and changed into an airy white sundress, barely looking at herself in the mirror. Now was not the time to care about beauty either. Now was the time for Sarah Whiteman to run for her life.

Sarah walked towards the port, feeling a chill run up her spine. The beach was vacant, not a single sound of life could be heard. Just the eeriness of the waves crashing against the sand, a sound that used to seem so relaxing and was now ominous and cold. She wondered why there weren't other tourists headed to the port. Was she the only one being saved? Surely, this boat wasn't just to save her and her alone. A local man greeted her on the port, a smile forming in the creases of his eyes.

"Good day ma'am," the man said joyously. "Are you ready to escape from the island of Zanzibar, this fine morning?"

"More than I ever could've thought imaginable," Sarah grimly replied, taking board onto the boat. "May I ask where I am headed? I am sure wherever it is that it will be a long boat ride."

The man laughed. "Not as long as you might think. We're headed to Prison Island. It's a short distance away from the mainland."

"Prison Island?!" Sarah shrieked. "Is this really all necessary? I'm just a tourist. I don't deserve to go to prison. I'm innocent. I swear!"

The man laughed again.

"No, no no," he reassured her. "Prison Island is not really a prison. It once was and that's why it is called that, but it isn't a prison anymore, ma'am."

"Well, that's reassuring," said Sarah, slowly calming down. "Correct me if I'm wrong, but I thought Zanzibar was the only island that had an airport. How am I going to get out of this place and back to the United States then?"

"Well, ma'am..." said the man as he walked to the front of the boat. "There's a man on Prison Island who requested that we bring you there in order to keep you safe. The arrangements will be made by him."

"Who is this man?" Sarah demanded. "What business does he have to make my arrangements?"

"You will find out in due time," said the man as he started the boat's engine. "My advice to you now would be to get on the boat and enjoy the ride. You can meet the man yourself and ask him this upon your arrival."

Sarah huffed at the man, placing her arms on her hips in anger, but knew that he was right. She'd better enjoy the ride and let him take her to Prison Island. What other option did she have? Sarah thought to herself that maybe this mysterious man might actually be Nikolai, to save her and make all of the bad go away.

"Nah..." Sarah muttered out loud, coming to her senses.

"A short distance away, my ass," thought Sarah hanging her head over the boat, watching the current rip against it. This had to be the longest boat ride of Sarah Whiteman's life. At least it seemed to be, anyways. Sarah felt like she was sitting on the boat for hours now, still finding no signs of life other than herself and the captain. Once in a while, the man driving the boat would turn around and flash a big smile at Sarah, but other than that, Sarah felt alone on this boat ride. Alone and left with only her thoughts-thoughts that were starting to terrorize her.

What if she wasn't actually being saved? What if these guerillas found out that Sarah worked for the Travel Connection and planned to use that against her? They could hold her hostage. It wouldn't be the first time that an American journalist was in the wrong place at the wrong time and became a pawn in some rebel game.

Sarah began to laugh at herself. Like hell Sarah Whiteman was of any importance to the United States. Last anyone knew Dee Dee was the star of Romantic Destinations, anyway. Nobody even knew who Sarah Whiteman was yet and surely nobody would really care to save her. Sarah Whiteman was pretty sure that if these guerillas were planning to hold her hostage on some desolate island, they wouldn't get anything for her. More than likely she wouldn't live, all because nobody knew who Sarah Whiteman was.

Sarah scoped out the man driving the boat. Was he one of them? He didn't look dangerous. He looked like a local man having fun transporting a tourist. He looked like he was doing his job, like he did every day. He looked happy. But maybe, Sarah thought, he was happy that he was transporting her because he was making enough to feed his family for the entire year. Maybe this man was happy because the guerillas were paying him well. Either way, this boat ride was taking a long time and Sarah was getting impatient.

"How much longer?" Sarah asked, slumping down into the seat.

The man laughed.

"Impatient, are we?" he teased, pointing his

finger towards the ocean. "See that small mound on the horizon? That's Prison Island, ma'am. We're almost there."

Sarah felt a rush of relief flood through her body. She could see Prison Island and could feel her anticipation settle down. "Free at last?" she thought to herself. "Or a prisoner on an island aptly named Prison Island? Time can only tell, Sarah. Time can only tell."

The man pulled up to the port singing an island tune, something about having fun in the sun, something Sarah once would have enjoyed hearing. At this point, it was beginning to cause a knot in her stomach. She began to grab her luggage, but the man stopped her, picking up her bags, instead. Sarah kindly thanked him and started to walk up the path from the port.

"The residence is at the top of the hill," said the man behind her. "I'll leave your bags once we reach the top and then I must be on my way."

"So you're not coming with me?" asked Sarah, the pit in her stomach growing larger. "How do I know that this is safe? You take me to this island in the middle of nowhere; you tell me nothing of the man who wants to save me. How do I know that this is not part of the guerillas' plan? How do I know that I am not being held hostage?"

"You don't know," said the man. "All you can do is trust me. You should also trust the man that you are going to meet. He does not mean you any harm and will ensure your safety. Good day, ma'am. I'll leave your bags with you now. I must get going while it is still safe."

Sarah looked around and realized that they had reached the top of the hill. Before she could say goodbye to the man, she saw her bags at her ankles; the man was already half way down the hill. It was too late to run now; Sarah just had to take her chances. So she grabbed her bags and continued walking the path towards a residence that looked more luxurious than any of the resorts she had seen on the main island. Whoever this man was, he sure was rich.

Beautiful, tropical plants surrounded the entrance of the home. Sarah could tell that whoever lived in this palace obviously had a landscaper, as every plant was perfectly placed and trimmed. In all of Sarah's career working with rich clients and customers, this had to be the most splendid house she had ever seen, so beautiful that Sarah almost forgot about entering the building and finding the man who was going to ensure her safety. She just stood for a while, admiring its beauty, until she heard a door open and saw a tall, handsome man come to greet her.

"Nikolai?" Sarah squealed, as the gentleman came towards her.

"Sarah, my beautiful doll!" the man exclaimed, opening his arms and embracing her with a big hug. "I'm so excited to see you and I'm glad that you're alright. Everything is okay. You'll be safe here and I promise a flight back to the US within a day or two."

Sarah withdrew from Nikolai's hug. She stood back and stared at him, coming out of her shock. Back on the island, she knew that Nikolai was wealthy. You could tell by his appearance. But she never imagined he was this wealthy. Not that wealth mattered, really; Sarah was just happy to see him. She felt like weeks had gone by since she'd seen a familiar face and seeing his gorgeous face was more than she ever hoped for.

"Shall we?" Nikolai asked, taking Sarah by the arm.

"My bags..." Sarah began to say, but Nikolai interrupted her, telling her not to worry, his servants would bring them to her room.

Half an hour passed before Nikolai finally reached the room that Sarah would be staying in. He showed her every single room in his house, all of which were extravagant and lavishly decorated. Sarah's room did not differ. The room, like all of the others in his house, was immaculate and well furnished. Clean design, rich whites and blues, and a king-sized bed all for Sarah's comfort.

Nikolai kissed Sarah ever so gently on her forehead. "I must go now. Please make yourself comfortable. Feel free to walk around the house and the island if you like."

"Wait...you're leaving?" Sarah asked, a fury burning in her eyes.

Nikolai smiled at Sarah. "Yes, I have important business to take care of, darling. I won't be gone for long. I'll meet you for dinner tonight at eight."

"But I have so many questions to ask you,

Nikolai," pleaded Sarah. "How am I getting home? How am I...?"

Nikolai put a finger on Sarah's eager lips. "Be patient, my darling. We will talk of everything tonight. Just try to enjoy yourself, okay?"

"Ok," said Sarah plainly, her eyes sorely looking at the floor rather than Nikolai.

Nikolai let out a laugh, picking Sarah up and squeezing the life out of her. "Dinner tonight, Sarah, we will talk. For now, enjoy yourself. You deserve it." And with that, he walked away, taking a turn at the end of the hall, and leaving Sarah again, alone with her thoughts.

Sarah didn't know whether she should unpack her bags or leave them. She wasn't quite sure what Nikolai had in store for her, nor was she sure when, if ever, she would be leaving this island. She decided she would unpack, if only because the beautifully curved armoire was just screaming to hold her things. The master bathroom that held a marble vanity was dying for her makeup brushes and night cream. Sarah may have had a terrifying experience on Zanzibar that left her with the inability to fully enjoy herself, but Nikolai told her to enjoy herself on his island and Sarah was going to do just that.

Like the hotel that Sarah stayed at on the island, the room that Nikolai had given her had two French doors that led outside. They led out to a stunning patio with a great view of the beach. Sarah was living the life of luxury; she decided she was going to order a glass of wine, and try to relax for a while.

Sarah daydreamed about living here with Nikolai, making love on the sand of the white beach, having butlers and servants to wait on them while they lived a life of excitement. Just as Sarah was being taken away, reality began to sink in. Did Sarah even know this man? The day before she despised him for leaving her feeling used and abused, but today she found herself thinking about living the rest of her life with him. Snap out of it, her mind pleaded.

Anger began to fill Sarah's veins. She was angry about this whole situation, but to make things worse, she was angry that Nikolai acted as if nothing happened. With money like this, he probably had sex with random women all the time. With money like this, Sarah probably didn't mean anything to him at all. She wasn't even sure that he had really saved her. The guerillas on the island seemed like they were of Russian decent. Perhaps, Sarah thought, Nikolai might be one of them. Perhaps he planned to use her as a hostage. And even if he wasn't, how did he have the ability to save her and send her home? There was obviously more about Nikolai than Sarah knew and everything about it smelled fishy. Sarah decided that she wasn't going to meet Nikolai for dinner that night after all. She was going to stay in her room and avoid him. If he wanted to talk to her, he'd come find her.

Sarah sat in her room; hours passed

27

without Nikolai coming to find her. The nerve of this man, to leave Sarah like this. As the blood begin to boil underneath Sarah's skin, she decided she was going to get answers and she was also going to let this man know that he hurt her like no man had ever hurt her before.

The dining room that Nikolai showed Sarah earlier in the day was empty. No sign of Nikolai's presence was there. Sarah felt even angrier. What if Nikolai never even showed up for dinner? Her head began to spin. Sarah had no idea where to find him.

"Is there something I can do for you, ma'am?" a young servant girl asked behind Sarah, startling her.

"Oh my!" Sarah squeaked, turning around to see the girl carrying dishes. "I'm sorry, you scared me. I'm looking for Nikolai. Any idea on where he might be?"

"Yes," said the girl with a large smile on her face. "Mr. Petroff was looking for you. He was rather upset that you didn't come to dinner tonight, but thought you might have taken a nap. He told us that if we saw you to direct you to his quarters. He would be spending the rest of the night there. Can I get you something to eat first? We have lobster bisque to start."

"No, thank you," said Sarah, excusing herself. "But thank you for your kindness. I'll go look for Nikolai."

Sarah raced up the stairs to the top floor. She walked towards Nikolai's room, feeling emotions ranging from anger, to fear, to sadness. Sarah didn't know quite how she felt; all she knew was that she wanted to confront him. She wanted an apology and she wanted answers. Nikolai was going to tell Sarah what was going on and he was going to get her on a plane as far away from this place as possible. She wanted to go home and she wanted to go home now. So without even bothering to knock, Sarah entered the room, finding Nikolai in front of a mirror with just a towel wrapped around his waist.

Damn, he looked good.

"You didn't come to dinner," Nikolai said calmly, not an ounce of surprise on his face.

Sarah stood still in shock. All of the thoughts that she had racing through her head before reaching Nikolai's room had vanished. All Sarah could think about was how good the man looked in front of her, wrapped in a towel that didn't quite hide the details of his large Russian cock. Nothing was left to Sarah's imagination, other than what she wanted to do to the handsome man that stood before her.

"I didn't," said Sarah, snapping back to reality. "I didn't want to."

"Were you not hungry?" asked Nikolai as he walked towards Sarah, leaning towards her cheek and finishing his question with a kiss.

"No," stammered Sarah. "I've been thinking and..."

Nikolai interrupted her words by moving his mouth to her lips, kissing her passionately.

Sarah could smell his clean scent; he must have just showered, she decided, after running her hands through his wet, dark hair. This man was sexy. Sarah didn't mind if she couldn't think anymore. She didn't remember that he left her that night at the hotel, feeling hurt. All Sarah could think about was how wild this man made her. Heat spread up her lower body, leaving a trail of fire that burned in her nipples. She wanted him.

"God, Sarah..." whispered Nikolai as he interrupted their kiss. "You're so beautiful in that dress. You're the most beautiful woman I have ever had the pleasure of making love to. I know that I left the hotel that night and there is much left to say, but I want you. Please tell me that I can have you, Sarah."

"I'm yours, Nikolai," moaned Sarah as she licked up his muscular neck, circling her tongue underneath his ear. "Make me yours."

Nikolai groaned. Sarah was making his dick so hard; he couldn't bear the small talk anymore. He licked her neck in return, biting into its flesh playfully, leaving Sarah whimpering with desire. He gently slid his hands down to her legs, rubbing up and down her voluptuous, perfectly trim thighs, gently pulling the bottom of her dress and lifting it off her body. Sarah stood there naked, her nipples erect from the sudden cool air pressed against her skin. Nikolai buried his face in her breasts, teasing her by licking everywhere but her erect nipples.

"I can't take it," cried Sarah.

Nikolai smiled, dropping down to his knees, his hands reaching up and pulling her hardened nipples. Sarah let out a moan and Nikolai let go. He took off her panties and opened the folds of her hot cunt, first playing with her clit and then placing his stiff tongue into her juicing pussy. Sarah leaned against the wall, moaning with pleasure. She placed her hands on her hard nipples and started pulling them. The orgasm came on strong; to increase it Sarah pulled her hand off her tit and used it instead to rub her clit as she came. She roared in satisfaction and Nikolai smiled up at her, while wiping her cum off his face.

"Your turn," Sarah said, smiling coyly at him.

Nikolai stood against the wall and this time Sarah lowered herself to her knees. She examined his large dick with her tongue, loving the clean taste of his freshly showered body. She slid her tongue playfully up and down his shaft, landing at his balls. She gently suckled on them, placing both hands on his dick as Nikolai moaned in ecstasy. Nikolai looked like he couldn't handle her teasing anymore, so Sarah moved her mouth onto his hot cock. She bobbed up and down on it, licking the sides of it like an ice cream cone. Nikolai just stood there moaning, watching her take him in between her pretty red lips.

"You're so good at that," he moaned while looking down at her. "Just watching you do that is making me want to cum. Let me put this dick in you, I don't want to explode in your mouth."

Sarah gave Nikolai's large member one last

lick and pulled herself up.

"To the bed?" she asked.

"No," said Nikolai, picking her up. "On the wall."

Nikolai pressed Sarah's back against the wall, lifting her up and down on his erect cock. Sarah aided him by jumping up and down on it, fingering her pussy the whole time. This made Nikolai even more excited, so he pressed his dick into her harder. He was so big that filling her up all the way in itself was making her orgasm. She wailed and threw the backs of her arms against the wall.

"I'm cumming!" she screamed. "I'm going to cum all over that fat dick of yours!"

Nikolai pressed his lips hard into Sarah, feeling the pleasures of her orgasm vibrating in his mouth. He pumped into her even harder, faster, feeling her pussy muscles contract against his cock. His body couldn't take it anymore and he released his warm cum inside of her. The two of them moaned together, slowing down their movements until they came to a complete stop. Nikolai pulled out of Sarah and laid down on his bed, patting the empty side next him.

"Lie in bed with me tonight," he said, pulling the luxurious satin sheets over his nude body and then over Sarah's as she laid down. "Stay in bed with me forever, Sarah. I don't ever want to let you go again."

Sarah looked up at him with her big, brown eyes. She smiled and relaxed back onto his chest. She let out a sigh, closed her eyes, and fell asleep to the sound of Nikolai's beating heart.

The sound of tropical birds singing woke Sarah from her peaceful slumber. She opened her eyes and could tell by the dimness of the sky that it was still early, perhaps six or seven in the morning. She reached her hand across the bed to feel for Nikolai. A familiar feeling sunk deep within her stomach, as she realized that Nikolai was, once again, not lying beside her. She jumped out of bed, putting on her dress from the night before. She was going to track Nikolai down and see why the hell he left her. She was going to find him and get the answers she forgot about last night. She felt stupid, thinking to herself that Nikolai had used his attractiveness to seduce her. How could she of fallen for him again? Sarah rushed out of the bedroom determined to face Nikolai head on, only to knock heads with him on her way out of the door.

"Sarah, where are you going?" Nikolai asked, while rubbing the sore spot on his head where it knocked against Sarah's.

"To find you," Sarah said flustered. "I thought for sure you left me again."

Nikolai laughed. "Sarah, darling, I was making breakfast arrangements for us. I originally planned to serve you breakfast in bed, but since you're awake, let's have breakfast in the dining room. Shall we?"

"I want answers," said Sarah strongly. "Enough of this bullshit, I just want answers Nikolai."

Nikolai's smile changed. He was taken aback by Sarah's demeanor. He knew that he had to give her the truth eventually, he had no other choice. He just didn't expect to see the hurt in her eyes. She looked as though he had crushed her spirit and Nikolai couldn't bear to see it. He was starting to love this woman. The last thing he ever wanted to do was hurt her.

"And I owe you them," said Nikolai, brushing her cheek with his hand. "I will tell you everything, I promise. But let's do it over breakfast, okay?"

The table was beautifully arranged with a spread that was to die for. Eggs Benedict, garden vegetables tossed in butter sauce with fresh herbs, little pieces of white fish and handmade rolls offered with a variety of butters and jellies. "It must be nice to have people who cook like this for you," Sarah thought as she remembered that most of her breakfasts for herself consisted of stale bread and some sort of processed cereal. She never was much of a cook.

They sat and talked for a while, buttering their rolls and chatting about how great of a cook Nikolai's chef was. Sarah was enjoying the breakfast and Nikolai's company so much that she forgot again about finding the answers she was looking for. Something about being with this man felt so right, almost as if she had been with him all of her life.

Over breakfast, Sarah Whiteman forgot

that she was a journalist who worked for Travel Connection. She forgot that guerillas took over Zanzibar and she forgot that she was saved by a knight in shining armor. Sarah Whiteman looked into Nikolai's eyes as if she had always been here with him on Prison Island, as if she had always been his woman, perhaps his wife. Sarah, sipping her glass of Sauvignon Blanc and inhaling the crisp island air, forgot everything until Nikolai brought up her unanswered questions.

"Sarah, darling," started Nikolai, interrupting the moment of silence the two shared between bites. "There are some things about me that I think you need to know."

"Oh, yes..." Sarah hesitated, startled by the interruption. "Yes, I believe there are."

"I've avoided telling you these things at first because I didn't want you to know about them, at least not yet. It's a rather long story, but I'll try to make it short." Nikolai continued, pausing to finish his last glass of wine.

"I come from a rich father. One who likes owning everything that money can buy. One who always wants more and never has enough. My father owns this. He bought Prison Island for me as a graduation present years ago. That was just the start of it, though. He started buying up chains of islands for private use, wanting to use a lot of them for resorts and tourism. He's a man of business and is always looking for a way to bring in profits. Which was fine, it was a great idea and a very successful one at that. But the man went crazy. He simply went mad, Sarah."

Sarah looked puzzled. There was a look of despair on Nikolai's once joyous face. His eyes looked down at the table, rather than meet her gaze.

"What's wrong, Nikolai?" she asked, trying to pry out the truth. "What does your father's madness have to do with the dangerous rebel situation on Zanzibar?"

Nikolai drew in a heavy breath.

"Sarah, he wanted to buy as much of the world that money could buy. He started as a man of respect and decency and turned into a power hungry monster. He didn't care about the local inhabitants of the islands or the countries that owned them. He'd kill everyone if it meant owning the islands."

"So he wanted Zanzibar?" Sarah asked, piecing the puzzle together. "He sent guerillas here to take over the island?"

"I sent guerillas there," responded Nikolai, correcting Sarah's suspicion. "I, too, was beginning to think like my father. I, too, wanted the island to be mine, no matter what the outcome. But all that..."

Sarah stood up, shaking, unable to control her anger.

"Your father is the monster?" she asked. "No, Nikolai. You are the monster! You terrorized the tourists. You terrorized the locals. And you terrorized me and my camera crew. You ruined the first real chance I ever had to make something of myself. And then you thought you were doing me a favor by bringing me to your island, while hell was continuing on Zanzibar? You may be attractive and charming Nikolai, and maybe that's enough to seduce a woman, but I will not be with a man who thinks of destruction for profit. That's dirty, that's dangerous, and I want nothing to do with it. You get me on a plane the hell out of Zanzibar and you get me a plane now! I'm going to my room to pack my bags. You have that plane ready for me."

"But...But..." Nikolai stammered. "Sarah, just listen..."

"There's nothing left to say," Sarah huffed, placing her hands on her hips. "Goodbye, Nikolai."

There was a knock at the door. Sarah hesitated for a few minutes to answer it, thinking that Nikolai would try to come up and talk her out of her decision. For once since the takeover of the island, Sarah felt powerful. She felt like she finally had the ability to make a decision of her own again, without judgment clouded by lust.

Nikolai might have been a great lover. Hell, she may have at one point wanted to spend the rest of her life with this man, but all of that whimsical thinking was gone now. Sarah remembered that she had a life. She had a life back home with family and friends. She had a career; granted, it was currently ruined, but she could more than likely piece it back together again once she got home. There were plenty of other fish in the sea that Sarah could catch. Fish that weren't dangerous, power-hungry liars. There was not a part of her mind that wanted Nikolai. Their affair was done, just a silly dream that Sarah would soon forget.

Feeling empowered by her thoughts, Sarah decided she'd get the door. Even if Nikolai was there, she now had the ability to tell him off. He wouldn't be able to seduce her this time. But when Sarah answered the door, she saw no signs of Nikolai. There was a young man beaming up at Sarah, flashing his pearly white teeth.

"Plane's ready, ma'am," said the man. "Nikolai has arranged the boat to take you to Zanzibar. From there you will be escorted by limo to the airport. A private jet will fly you to Africa and from there you have arrangements to take the plane back to the United States."

"Thank you," replied Sarah, grabbing her bags. "I can't wait."

The local man who originally brought Sarah to Prison Island was waiting for her with a flashing smile at the port. Sarah, who originally viewed the man as mysterious and untrustworthy, now found serenity in his presence. This man meant that Sarah was finally going home. This man meant that this nightmare was finally over with.

The boat ride didn't seem as long this time around. In fact, it flew by Sarah in a blink of an eye. She chatted up her travel companion, not about danger or rebels, but about local lore, music and family. Sarah couldn't wait to see her family; she dreamed of her mother and father's embrace. She wondered if they even knew she was in danger on the island of Zanzibar.

The small talk made Sarah forget about some of the details of the last few days, but there was something that kept finding its way into Sarah's thoughts. She kept trying to push it away, thinking about back home or the weather, anything that would keep it away. Sarah just couldn't bear to think about Nikolai. She couldn't bear to think about heading back to Prison Island, starting over, forgetting the whole thing. Most of all she couldn't stop thinking about why Nikolai never came to see her, why he never came to say goodbye. Was she really that meaningless to him? He didn't even fight for her to stay.

At the airport on Zanzibar, Sarah took one last look around at the island that once was. She came to the island with so many aspirations and dreams, only to become a slave to a man who overpowered her with charisma and sex. Sarah bit her lip while walking towards the jet. God, the sex was great. She had to admit that.

She started to walk up the stairs to the plane, still secretly fuming with anger. Why didn't Nikolai at least have the decency to say goodbye? Perhaps he didn't plan to win her over. Perhaps she didn't mean too much to him, but didn't he have the decency to at least say goodbye? After all, he did ruin her life the last few days.

"Sarah!" yelled a voice from out of nowhere. "Wait!"

Sarah turned around, recognizing the familiar face.

"Nikolai?" she asked in surprise. "What are you doing here?"

"Sarah…" Nikolai stammered, almost out of breath. "I can't let you go. I just can't."

"Nikolai," Sarah started. "I'm not just some piece of property like Zanzibar. I'm a human being and I have a voice. I have a mind. I have a life, Nikolai. I have a real life in Buffalo, a life that I plan on going back to, forgetting that this whole thing happened. What we had was fun, it was exciting, but I didn't know you. I didn't know anything about you, but now I do. And to be honest Nikolai, now that I do, I have no reason to stay here with you. You're a criminal and a crook and you are not somebody that I want to be with."

"I was," replied Nikolai. "I was a criminal. I was a crook, but all of that has changed Sarah. Don't you see you've changed me? You've changed me into a better person. You've reminded me of the person that I was before I became a power-hungry fool like my father. The humanitarian, a person who respects people other than myself. I respect you, Sarah, and I love you. I've never met a woman like you, someone who could change me the way you have. All of the women before you, Sarah, were nothing but a good time. But you are different. You're intelligent and caring. We can talk about almost anything. I can open up to you, even though I bury my emotions. I can open up to you, Sarah. I love you and I know I'll never in my life meet another woman who can change me the way you have. Sarah, please stay. Please stay and be my wife."

"Your wife?" Sarah interrupted. "Are you kidding me, Nikolai? We barely know each other and I'm not sure I can even trust you. Not to mention that I would have to leave the life that I have in the United States for you. My family, my friends, my career...for you?"

Nikolai dropped down to one knee, opening a small box that held a white gold ring embedded with diamonds.

"Sarah Whiteman, please be my wife," he begged. "I don't want Zanzibar. I want the locals to keep their beloved island. But Prison Island is rightfully mine and I want us to live together there. The island is big enough that we could move your family there, build them houses if you would like. I have millions of dollars and so many businesses, money would never be a problem for us. You would never have to work again. We could travel the world. We could visit family and friends whenever you chose. I'll provide everything for you, Sarah. I'll take every single worry that you have away. I just need you. I need you to be my wife."

Sarah stood on the steps frozen, her jaw half open in shock. She had never been proposed to. Sarah never even had a boyfriend serious enough to think about marrying. Yet here she was, standing ten feet away from a man that she had known for only a few days, a few terrible days at that, and she wanted to marry him. Sarah Whiteman wanted to become Mrs. Sarah Petroff.

"I love you, Nikolai," she beamed, running down the stairs to embrace him. "I want to become your wife. I never want to leave you again."

The two locked lips for what seemed like hours. Sarah could swear that she heard the hums of angels circling around them. The moment was perfect. Sarah never wanted to leave this moment. She wanted to keep her lips glued forever against Nikolai's, but as she felt the stiffness inside his pants press against her, she decided she had other plans in mind.

"Nikolai..." she began, unlocking from their kiss and looking at him slyly. "Since you have already purchased this plane, how about we use it?"

"For what?" he asked unknowingly.

Sarah smiled at him, with passion burning in her eyes.

"Oh, I get it," he responded with a laugh. "That's my naughty wife."

"You know, Nikolai," said Sarah as they boarded the plane, entering a lush entertainment area set with a bed and bottles of champagne. "You hurt me a lot in the beginning of this relationship. I think you owe me."

"Yes," replied Nikolai dimly. "I owe you the whole world."

"The world? Now, Nikolai, you know what I think about being power hungry," she replied teasingly. "But I see nothing wrong with you allowing me to dominate you a little. For all of that fear, I think you owe me a little pleasure."

"I think I do," said Nikolai hungrily.

"Then come over here," said Sarah, lying down on the bed and spreading her legs. "Come eat my pussy. It's already soaking wet, waiting for you."

"Gladly," replied Nikolai, getting down on his knees before her.

Nikolai put his hands up her dress to pull down her panties, only to find out she wasn't wearing any. The idea of this made him even hungrier for her dripping snatch, so he decided to dive right in. Pulling apart her pussy lips, he flicked his tongue against her hardened clit, and then circled it down into her hot hole pushing it in and out of her. Sarah was moaning in pleasure, finding the sensation of his tongue almost unbearable. She felt like any minute now she could squirt her milky fluids all over his clean-shaven face.

"Fuck me hard with your tongue," she demanded. "I'm going to cum all over that face of yours."

Nikolai stiffened his tongue and pulled it in and out of her soaking pussy even faster. He could feel her muscles clenching and knew she was going to cum once she lifted her hips off the bed, pressing them into his mouth. She let out a scream, squirting cum all over his lips and chin.

"That was good," she said. "But I think you deserve a little torture now."

Before Nikolai could respond, Sarah got up and pinned him to the bed. She licked his lips then sucked on his tongue, licking it and sucking on it as if it was his dick. Nikolai wanted her mouth on his dick right then and there, but Sarah had other plans. She licked down his chest instead, tracing her tongue around his nipples, then taking them into her mouth and biting them slightly. Nikolai moaned in pleasure, still wishing her magical mouth was on his throbbing member, which she still didn't even lay a hand on.

Sarah looked into Nikolai's eyes, flashing him a foxy smile. She knew she was teasing him, making him internally beg for her mouth on his cock, but she wasn't giving in. This was torture, right? She continued licking him, swirling her tongue down his flat abs until she reached his dick. Nikolai almost jumped out in excitement, dying to maneuver her head onto his cock, but decided to let her continue with her torture instead. Rather than touch his cock with her tongue, Sarah slid it down one thigh, then up to the next. She grabbed his balls and gently squeezed them with a free hand. She lifted her head off of his thighs, and while looking up at him, gently licked his balls. Nikolai closed his eyes and moaned in ecstasy.

While Nikolai's eyes were closed, Sarah planned her assault. She took her tongue off his balls, stood up and sat on his dick-backwards, with her juicy ass facing him. She took his full cock in, riding him back and forth. The intensity of the sensation made him want to cum instantly, but he held it, wanting to save it for her. She stopped abruptly and decided to bounce up and down on it rather than ride it to and fro. Nikolai grabbed the bubbly ass that was happily bouncing in front of him.

"You can torture my dick all you want, Sarah," he said, while heavily breathing. "But I'm going to torture that thick ass of yours."

Sarah moaned. She had to admit that as much as she liked dominating him, she enjoyed being submissive to him even more. Especially when he talked dirty to her like that and took full control. She bounced up and down even harder on his fat cock. She felt like she was going to burst any second now. Nikolai firmly grabbed her ass cheeks, slapping one at a time, watching the aftershock of a sexy jiggle that followed. He felt her pussy contract on his cock as her white cream covered it, as she continued to jump up and down. He slapped her ass one last time, hearing her moan in pleasure.

Sarah was starting to tire and slow her pace, so Nikolai grabbed her ass and took full control. He bobbed her up and down, pounding the life out of her already swollen pussy. He felt his dick stiffen a little and he let out a final moan as he shot his thick wad into her cunt.

Their bodies lay spent next to one another on the bed. Sarah shifted her body and rested on Nikolai's chest, hearing him inhale and exhale feverishly, their faces both beaming.

"Nikolai," Sarah said, after laying there in silence for a while. "Can we go home now? I'd like you to meet my family. I want to surprise my parents with the good news."

"Of course we can, beautiful," said Nikolai, rubbing his still-stiffened cock. "But first, I need you to do something for me."

"Sure, babe," replied Sarah. "Anything for

you."

"Well, I let you get away with torturing me earlier, babe. But I need your mouth on my cock, now."

"Geez, Nikolai," Sarah teased. "Don't you ever get enough?"

"No Sarah, not at all," replied Nikolai. "Till the day we die together, I will never have enough of you."

2 LOVE AS NO PRICE TAG

The coldness of the floor in the empty bathroom almost felt as cold as Kelly Fontanne's heart. She looked in the mirror at her own reflection, researching the new nightgown she had bought for the special occasion. Frankie was going to just die. She looked as ravishing as she thought she would be when she ordered the nightgown online. It hugged each of her slender curves in all of the right places, and the thin fabric that perfectly hugged the outlines of her breasts made them look bigger than they really were.

"Knock him dead," Kelly thought to herself, as she sat on the toilet, placing each of her two feet into the tiny black pumps.

Frankie lay on her bed, his two arms behind his head, grinding into Kelly's fluffy pillows. He teased his half-risen cock that hid between the fabrics of his jeans. It wasn't a matter of what Kelly was wearing; it was obvious that she was hot, but Frankie had to admit that he loved waiting for her in anticipation. Each outfit perfectly showcased her body, the excitement making him lust for her like a wild animal.

Kelly and Frankie had been sharing nights with one another for some time now. They originally met at a club that Frankie was "DJ-ing" at and ended up having a one-night stand. The sex the two shared with each other was too good for either to just leave the experience at one night. They continued seeing each other each night for months now.

Frankie loved the fiery inferno that he has seen in Kelly's eyes. She was truly a woman who knew what she wanted and went after it. He admired her. After the first few months went by, Frankie started insisting that they move their sexual relationship into something more serious, but Kelly seemed to be hell-bent on not wanting a real relationship with him, or at all for that matter. She claimed to be too tied up with work; that her career stress was too demanding on her. She didn't want to throw a relationship into the mix and have something more to worry about. Although it broke Frankie's heart that he couldn't turn his relationship with his dream girl into something more, he was okay with settling for sexually pleasing her and himself.

Kelly got up off of the toilet and took one last look at herself in the mirror. She could barely see the outline of her thighs in the reflection but could tell by lifting off her height by two inches that her legs looked stunning in the pumps she was wearing. She took a deep breath and headed to the direction of the door. Once opening the door off of its closure, she saw the shadow of her male companion snooping in her stuff.

"What the fuck are you doing, Frankie?" she demanded, her eyes in the direction of the man digging through her dresser drawers.

"I...uh...was...just...looking for something," he stuttered, now turned around and showcasing a horrified look upon his face.

"Which was?" Kelly questioned, hands now positioned on angry hips.

"Look Kelly..." Frankie began. "You know I want you, girl. I know that you claim you have too much on your shoulders right now, but I worry that you're just seeing another man and don't want to tell me the truth."

Kelly looked at the sullen man and smiled, walking toward his direction. She walked behind him, putting one hand on his dick and the other across his mouth.

"Shhh..." she whispered sultry, hand now moving up and down his stiffened dick. "We're not dating, Frankie. My sexual business is not yours, just as yours is not mine. You understand that, don't you? I don't want our nights of passion to end just because of some silly misunderstanding."

"Uh huh," Frankie responded, barely able to breathe the words that came out of his mouth.

Kelly's hands were working miracles down on his cock. Who cares if she still didn't want something real? Frankie wasn't going to stop their erotic relationship now when she was doing all of this work. He stood in silence, gasping at the slippery hands sliding up and down on his cock.

"Good," Kelly said slyly, excusing herself off of Frankie's throbbing member and sitting down on the edge of her bed, her legs wide open. "Now come over here and lick this dripping, wet pussy."

Frankie's body stood motionless for a moment. He stared at the woman on the bed who was now moving her fingers in and out of her own pussy. Kelly wasn't wearing any panties under that red lace nightie of hers and the idea of that was making Frankie's cock want to explode. He smiled down at her and walked toward the bed, kneeling down once he came to a complete stop in front of her. He took his hand and rubbed her clit, watching as Kelly leaned back her head, moaning in ecstasy. Kelly was right; her pussy was sopping wet, ready for his cock to pound the daylight out of it.

Frankie leaned into her hot cunt, spreading its lips with both of his hands. The smell of Kelly's pussy was enough to make beads of precum form onto his dick. She smelled so sweet, like a ripe tropical fruit's nectar. He took his tongue and toyed with her clit, knowing that Kelly enjoyed being teased at first when he gave her oral. His eyes locked with hers, as he watched her pull her robust tits out of the lace nightie and play with her nipples. Watching her play with herself always turned Frankie on. He pulled his tongue off of her thickened clit and lowered down into her cum drizzling slit, pushing his tongue forcefully in and out of her hole. Kelly's hips bucked up and down on the bed, dancing on top of his tongue as if she were fucking it. She rode his mouth, feeling Frankie's tongue lick at her pussy hungrily. She let out a scream as she came all over his face, feeling her juices get licked up by his tongue. Frankie backed out from underneath her and looked up at the woman who now lay frozen on the bed.

"You're turn?" she asked cunningly, adjusting herself to sit back up on the bed.

"Yes, please," Frankie quickly answered, standing up with his dick as if it were going to solute her. "I love the feeling of your mouth on my hard cock."

Frankie leaned against the bed, pushing his cock toward Kelly's direction. Kelly lay on her stomach, ass in the air, admiring Frankie's cock. It was perfectly sculpted, with incredible girth that Kelly could not wait to feel fill her up. She leaned over, licking the tip playfully, continuing down the shaft. Frankie adjusted himself on his tiptoes, so he could feel her innocent tongue licking flirtatiously at his balls. Kelly sucked on each of them gently, taking little nibbles in at a time. She moved her arm underneath her body and inserted a finger into her cunt that still was gushing juices. She looked up at the large smirk that beamed across Frankie's face, keeping her eyes on his as she engulfed his entire cock into her mouth. Frankie let out a groan, slapping her ass with each motion of her head bobbing up and down. Her ass looked amazing as each ripple jiggled down to her thighs. In Frankie's opinion, Kelly had the hottest ass in the world.

Frankie moved his hips up and down,

intentionally slamming his cock in and out of Kelly's mouth. He knew she liked it rough; that's what he liked most about her in bed. Kelly began moaning loudly as she continued shoving her finger in and out of her cunt. As she began to feel her vaginal muscles clench and tighten, she removed her mouth off of Frankie's swollen member. If Kelly was going to cum again, it was going to be on his dick, not on her fingers. Kelly got up from lying down and sat on the bed in her knees.

"Sit down on the edge of the bed," Kelly demanded. "I want to fuck you while you sit."

Frankie happily did as he was told. He was always so compliant to each of Kelly's requests. He watched as Kelly positioned herself on top of his cock, placing her legs over each side of his thighs. She hopped up and down on his cock, uncontrollably, almost coming to climax as she felt his fingers wildly play with her clit. Kelly grabbed each of her tits in the palm of her hands, teasing the nipples with her fingers. Her pussy tightened on Frankie's thick Italian cock, making her moan out load with each explosion of her orgasm. She sat listless on his cock, as he took full control. He grabbed her hips, making her continue to bob up and down on his cock. Kelly could feel his dick becoming thicker, as it let go of its warm milk inside of her. The two sat, still inside of each other, panting their heavy breaths.

"That was amazing as always," Frankie exclaimed, kissing Kelly on her cheek.

"I love our sex," Kelly said breathlessly, smiling into Frankie's eyes.

"Fuck!" Kelly shouted, moving Frankie's arm off of her exhausted body and jumping out of bed. "It's 9:30, Frankie. I'm late for work; you have to go."

Frankie's eyes opened; he looked at the wrecked woman standing outside the other half of the bed. His dick was hard as a rock, watching the nude body that was affixed in front of him. They must've overslept, but she was going to be late anyways. He figured that he might as well take a chance and seduce her one last time before work.

"Do you know how sexy you look right now?" he asked her, letting out a yawn at the end of his question. "Why don't you come over here and sit on this cock. You're going to be late anyways, Kelly."

Kelly turned around and looked at Frankie, who was now playing with his cock underneath the bed sheet. She knew that she was late and shouldn't give in into his sexual powers, but watching Frankie pleasure himself was always such a turn-on and she was wet.

"I don't know Frankie," she teased. "If I fuck you now, I won't be an hour late. I'll be two."

"But it will be worth it, baby," Frankie said convincingly, uncovering his dick from the sheet.

Kelly walked over toward Frankie's side of the bed and took off her underwear. She kept her eyes on him as she got onto the bed and lowered her body onto his cock. His morning wood was always so full of life. Kelly knew once he asked her to fuck him, she wasn't going to say no. She couldn't deny this irresistible man.

Frankie took full command, grabbing Kelly by the hips and moving her back and forth onto his cock. Kelly hollered wildly as she let go of herself and came onto his dick. As much as Frankie wanted to make their sex last all morning, his first orgasm of the day was always the fastest. He took a free hand and ferociously rubbed her clit as she came. Watching her expression on her face made Frankie unable to control his orgasm. He let out a loud moan and came inside of her. Kelly lay on top of his chest, spent. Time sat between them.

"I really have to go to work," Kelly said while looking up into Frankie's half-closed eyes. "The sex was worth being late for, but you need to leave. I have to get ready."

"Ok babe," Frankie whispered sleepily. "Go hop in the shower; I'll be gone before you're done."

Kelly shot one last smile at Frankie and got up off of the bed. She gathered her work attire and headed toward her master bathroom, blowing one last kiss at the man who most satisfied her.

Being late for work was always such a bitch. Getting from Manhattan to the city always seemed to be more time-consuming than Kelly originally thought. She walked toward the direction of Indie Publishing Co., seeing its tall presence in the landscape. She pulled out her compact from her purse and took one last look at her face. Nobody would be able to tell what kind of mind-blowing night Kelly just had. She licked her lips and smiled, remembering the fun that she just had while sitting on top of Frankie's cock, and walked into the glass doors of the building.

"Kelly...Kelly!" exclaimed Vanessa, running toward the direction of Kelly's silhouette that was now jetting down the hallway. "Kelly, I need to talk to you!"

Kelly came to a quick halt, turning around to look at Vanessa, her Financial Director chasing her in what seemed like a rut. What now?

"Can I help you with something, Vanessa?" Kelly asked, as the frail woman approached her. "Did something happen?"

"No, nothing serious happened," Vanessa responded, trying to catch her breath. "You had a visitor earlier this morning though, another man from Smith & Welch Publishing Co."

Kelly stood inanimate and threw her hands into her face, where she covered a loud, irritated scream.

"When the fuck are these bastards going to get it?" she shouted. "I'm not selling Indie Publishing to them or to anyone else for that matter."

Vanessa walked over to the fire-blazon Kelly and wrapped her arm around her shoulder, walking her further down the hall.

"I know, I know, Kelly," she reassured her. "I told them that you wouldn't settle. They just keep bringing up the fact that we're facing a huge debt right now. They had a rather good proposition for us this time."

"I don't need their fucking proposition, Vanessa," Kelly angrily responded, brushing Vanessa's arm off of her shoulder. "What I need is a moment to breathe without some giant conglomerate breathing down my back."

"I don't like it as much as you don't," Vanessa said dimly. "But I, like you and everyone here at Indie Publishing, love my career. I don't want to see this company fall down to the ground and Smith & Welch offered not only the half mill but also a guarantee that no employees would be fired. I think you should just hear them out. They want to meet with you tomorrow."

"God damn it," Kelly shouted, racing ahead of the sore Vanessa that fell behind her. "I'll meet with Smith & Welch tomorrow, alright? But everything is going to be on my terms, not theirs!"

"I'll let them know," Vanessa promised, now walking in a complete opposite direction from Kelly who was headed to her office. "And don't worry Kelly. I know that your terms will win the deal."

Kelly slammed her office door behind her. What nerve of Smith & Welch to keep trying to buy up Indie Publishing! Who in the hell did they think they were? Who in the hell did Vanessa think she was trying to set up this meeting with them tomorrow? It was Kelly who was the CEO after all, not Vanessa, and not some lame brain from Smith & Welch.

Kelly sat at her office desk aimless for some time, trying to avoid the anger she felt by completing useless tasks on her desktop. She had to admit that Indie Publishing was going down the tubes. The company, mostly at her end, took too many risks on the marketing of these last authors, and here they were left standing in debt to a marketing failure rather than making profits on their works. She tried everything she felt was possible to turn the company back around and watch their figures skyrocket up rather than further down, but she failed. She didn't want to lose her company; all of the people she loved and cherished worked hard for their positions there. She didn't want to be the one to take them all away from their careers. She bit nervously down on the eraser of a pencil, contemplating what in the world her terms would be at the meeting. She really couldn't put much at stake being that the company was already half a million dollars in debt, but she could put up the one thing she had faith in—her body.

Kelly leaned back into her office chair and mapped out her plans inside of her head. She didn't want Smith & Welch to own the company, but they did have the financial stability to help her get out of her debt. What she wanted to do was to make them a partner, not an owner, getting them to partially own their name and works and supplying the money to get out of debt in return. Kelly thought of the men she had been propositioned with by the company. All of them were young, good-looking guys. It would be a piece of cake to get them to agree to loan her half a million dollars with only a partnership in return for sex. Hell, if Kelly had too, she'd take three or four of those guys at once. She loved Indie Publishing and she'd do whatever it would take to keep the company in her hands.

Jersey. God, the worst thing about this company was that it was located in Jersey. Kelly hated everything about the place; in her mind it didn't just stink literally, but it stunk physically just viewing it. Kelly couldn't remember why she hated New Jersey. She just knew that she despised it and avoided it at all costs until today.

Meeting with a member from Smith & Welch was going to be tough. Although Kelly knew just exactly what she was going to bribe them with, she still felt the nervousness in her stomach rumble. She may have been secretly provocative between the sheets outside of work, but that was with men she knew, men who usually asked her first.

She took a big gulp as she walked into the revolving door of the high-class downtown hotel. She felt the eyes of sharply dressed businessmen checking her out as she made her way toward the lobby to check in. Pigs, she thought. All men are pigs, with the same thing in the back of their minds. Winning the heart of the representative from Smith & Welch was going to be easy, no matter how anxious the whole thing was starting to make her feel.

Kelly gave the attractive lobbyist one last big flash of her pearly whites and made her way to her hotel room. The ride on the elevator seemed like it was taking forever to reach her room on the 20th floor. The air of the hotel was stale, but the room was extraordinaire. Guilt stemmed over Kelly's mind as she realized all of her suite was being funded by the company. Here she needed a handout but at the same time had her secretary order her the most luxurious room the hotel could offer. Maybe, Kelly thought, Indie Publishing's going down in flames was all her fault. Maybe she just didn't know how to make a decent decision.

Kelly unpacked her bags and started to put her items onto the provided hangers in the closet when she pulled out the little black dress she was going to wear at today's meeting. The dress was defiantly going to knock the socks off of whomever they were sending to meet with her. With its body-hugging fabric and open lace neckline, there was no way her wearing the dress wouldn't make the gentleman a bit uncomfortable to begin with.

Kelly beamed in delight, holding the dress in front of her. Something about this, although so foreign, made her feel so damned sexy—being in power, taking control of an unaware victim, and mostly getting what she wanted in the end without much damage to herself, her employees, or the company. She felt that wetness started to form in the crease of her panties. She hadn't had much time that morning to take a shower or get ready for the day, so with two hours to loose, Kelly decided she was going to take a shower and pleasure herself at the same time.

This hotel room really was a luxury, set with a Jacuzzi and shower handle that seemed like it has just the right amount of water pressure. Kelly quickly got out of her jeans and tee, standing in just her underwear and admiring herself in the bathroom mirror. Her tits were perfect—big, beautiful, gigantic in comparison to her tiny waist. She turned around and took a glimpse at her flawless ass in the mirror, which seemed to be begging for room between the black laced thong that she was wearing. Her body was perfect; there was no way that the man she'd seduce would turn her down, even if he was married.

Kelly placed her hands around the fullness of each breast, gently tugging her nipples, feeling the sensations of sex running throughout her body. She loved having her breasts teased, as it always seemed to make her pussy instantly flood with its own juices. She walked toward the Jacuzzi and sat into it, feeling the pressure of its jets harshly rushing against her body. The pressure from just the water hitting across her flesh was making her want to instantly cum. Kelly kept a hand on her nipple, teasing it, and placed her other hand onto her clit. She moaned in her own personal gratification, rubbing her clit intensely. Kelly wanted to feel the sensation of both her nipples being tugged at the same time. She sat up in the Jacuzzi onto her knees and pressed her pussy against the jet that was forcefully streaming water. She rocked her hips back and forth against the current, feeling herself cum as she pulled at her nipples one last time.

Kelly laughed to herself and lay back down in the tub. She was such a horny girl. She was ready to blow away whatever businessman would soon sit beside her. Kelly quickly washed up and threw on the black dress. She spent the rest of her time getting ready for the sexy meeting she was soon going to encounter.

Rico obviously was used to catering to these types of customers. When Kelly walked into the restaurant, the first thing the greeter asked was who she was going to meet with that night. Kelly was taken by surprise but quickly mumbled that she didn't know the name of the person, but that she was meeting with a representative from Smith & Welch.

"Ah yes...," the greeter responded, not even wasting time looking at the list of reservations that sat before him. "Oliver is waiting for you. He seemed a bit bothered that you are late. He's been checking on your arrival every five minutes."

"I had a hard time finding the place," Kelly responded.

"That's okay. Follow me," the greater

continued, leading Kelly toward the direction of the dining area.

A pit formed inside Kelly's stomach, not because she was thirty minutes late or because she was going to take advantage of the man she was just about to meet, but because of his name. Oliver, the name seemed so familiar, so similar to a man she once knew. Of course, there had to be hundreds of thousands of Olivers in this world. Kelly would only be silly to think the Oliver she hated was going to be the man that she was meeting tonight.

The greeter reached the table, motioning for Kelly to sit down. Kelly, upon entering the full view of the table, was unable to see the face of the man until she sat across from him. She gasped at the sinful smile that beckoned back at her.

"Chardonnay for the lady," the man instructed, making a motion for the greeter to go away. "Hi Kelly! It's nice to see you."

"I wish I could say the same for you," Kelly responded angrily, looking down at the menu rather than at the man's face. "Who would've known that the obnoxious Smith & Welch would hire an even more obnoxious man like you?"

The man took a sip of spirits and laughed.

"Still got that hot-headed character, don't you, Kelly?" The man asked, in between sips. "I guess that was the reason why I always liked you."

Kelly looked up at the man with a sour look on her face.

"Did your company invite me for this

meeting with an attempt to win me over by having you represent them?" Kelly asked. "Because if they did, it was a poor decision. I'm never going to agree with whatever you put onto the table tonight. A few years may have passed Oliver, but I still despise your guts."

Oliver gulped down the last sip of his drink. He wore a straight face, showing Kelly no indentation that her cruel words affected him.

"Kelly, I'm meeting you here today because I am the last person who will be meeting you from Smith & Welch ever again." Oliver started, leaning in toward Kelly who sat across the table. "So that you know, I own Smith & Welch, well at least partially with my partner David Smith. I knew in the beginning that if I was the one who approached you about this business offer, I would've gotten a door slammed into my face. So instead, I sent five of my best men over to approach you and your company, all of whom got the door slammed into their faces. Now there's once chance left and the only one who is left to offer it to you is me."

Kelly sat across from Oliver in almost what seemed like complete hysteria. Had she gone mad? Last she knew of Oliver Welch was that he was the English professor who broke her heart without reason. His only reason at the time was that she was too young for him—that both of them were headed in different directions; but Kelly obviously wasn't too young to have a passionate affair with, and now here they sat in the same direction after all. This time, yet again, Oliver was in control of the cards.

"So you're in charge of the company, huh?" She questioned, after time sat between them. "Then tell me, Mr. Welch, what the hell do you want to do with Indie Publishing? Last I knew I was too 'young' to be part of your life, so you destroyed mine. And now here you are trying to destroy my life again by overtaking my company? Some nerve you have."

"Kelly...," Oliver pleaded. "I never tried to destroy your life and I'm not trying to destroy it now, let alone your company. For some time now, I've had great admiration for the publications that Indie produced, and when I heard that it was going under, I wanted to help get it back on its feet. When I found out that you are the company's CEO, I knew that because of our past, you wouldn't let me help you, but honestly, because of our past, that made me want to help you more. I love Indie Publishing, Kelly. Let me help you so that you don't lose your business."

Kelly slumped back into the restaurant's seat. She could not stand the man who sat across from her. His intentions may seem honest, but the hurt that he had put upon her in the past was enough to make her want to get up and leave. She frowned at her own thoughts, knowing that having sex with Oliver defiantly wasn't going to be the answer to settling this Smith & Welch scenario after all. Kelly would rather die knowing that she failed Indie Publishing before she let Oliver Welch save it, but then the thoughts of all of her faithful employees got in the way. She couldn't let them lose their jobs; she had to do whatever it took to keep the company afloat.

"Okay, Oliver," Kelly began. "What are you promising my company? I hope that you do know that I will never allow you to have complete control of its decisions. Let's just get that out of the way right now."

Oliver laughed, looking deeply into Kelly's eyes.

"You're still that fiery woman I used to know," he said, taking a new sip from the fresh drink the waiter had just poured.

"Cut the small talk," Kelly demanded. "We're here to talk business, not our past. The past is over, Oliver."

"I know, I know," he chuckled. "I just always loved your character. I'm glad to see that you haven't changed that about yourself."

Oliver cleared his throat, looking at the peeved woman sitting across from him.

"Business?" he asked, wearing a slick smile across his face. "It's quite simple really. You merge with my company; we bail you out. You get to keep your employees, you get to stay CEO of your company, and you get to make all of the decisions. The payback in return is pennies in comparison."

"And what's the payback?" Kelly questioned, taking a last sip of her Chardonnay and glancing at the couple sitting next to them.

Oliver sat in silence, toying at the answer inside of his mind.

"Well...,"he started, leaning in toward Kelly and almost whispering. "You pay back the loan with no interest over time. The money doesn't mean very much to me, if at all."

"Why are you whispering?" Kelly accused.

"If the payback of the money doesn't mean very much at all, why do you seem like there's something further up your sleeve?"

Oliver smiled at Kelly's questioning eyes.

"I want one night with you," he said abruptly. "Not necessarily sex, but I want to have an opportunity to make up for the wrong thing I did the first time."

"Goodbye Oliver," Kelly shouted, getting out from her chair and exiting the building.

The weekend had felt like the longest one Kelly had ever experienced in her life. The nerve of that man to just think he could enter her life again, offer her money for her troubled company, and then ask for a night to make up for the heart break he had caused in return. Kelly had no idea how else she was going to fund her company's debt, but surely anything would be better than spending one night alone with Oliver ever again.

Frankie had begged to come over to share a rendezvous night with Kelly again that Sunday, but Kelly had to turn him down. She was too stressed about the financial outcome of her company and she was too irritated having to have Oliver on her mind again. Instead, she chose to spend that Sunday night going to bed early and forgetting all of her troubles.

Monday felt like a chopping block that was waiting for Kelly's head. She knew upon entering the office that she would be greeted by a hundred of worried employees who hoped her meeting last Friday was the answer to their prayers. In turn, she would have to let them down and somehow convince them not to feel doubtful. Kelly pondered every excuse inside of her head, searching for any ounce of hope that she could find, but she had nothing. Kelly had a hollow mind to complement the void that she called her soul.

To Kelly's surprise, she was not greeted by her dutiful employees that morning at the front door but by two auditors instead— auditors who had turned her building and her office inside out in search of traces for the two million dollars that they claimed she owed them. Turns out, Kelly's accountant had been stealing money from her company all along. Here she was thinking all of this time that the debt was based on her poor decisions and publications, when really Tina was swindling for years.

Tina was much more intelligent than Kelly had originally thought. Somehow, she set the whole thing up to look like Kelly was her co-conspirator. No matter what excuse Kelly gave the auditors to make them believe that she wasn't part of it, she couldn't convince them. Kelly was going to need a damn good lawyer and a damn good lawyer fast. How the hell she was going to afford one though was the real question at hand.

Hours of interrogation had passed before Kelly found her scrunched-up body lying on her office floor, tears bleeding from her eyes. How could Tina do this to her, to the company? And how the hell was she going to afford to fight this?

Oliver Welch, although bleak, was her only choice now. She might have thought before that she'd rather watch her building fall to the ground before allowing his assistance, but right now the building was on fire and he was the only one who could put out the flames quick enough.

Kelly lifted her collapsed figure off of the office floor and crawled toward the phone that sat on top of her desk. She pulled out the card Oliver Welch had left to her and dialed the numbers that were given, wiping the tears from her eyes. She refused to let Oliver know just how vulnerable she was at this point.

"Oliver Welch speaking," Oliver answered in a cheerful, professional tone.

"Hello?" he asked, after a moment of silence passed by since his greeting.

Kelly cleared her throat and put a pretend smile upon her face.

"Hi, Oliver," she answered. "It's Kelly. Kelly Fontanne, how are you doing?"

"Well pretty okay," Oliver responded, still keeping a cheerful tone in his voice, although much more casual now. "Even after you left me last Friday, making me look like the biggest joke in the world."

"Yea, about that," Kelly hesitated while playing with the cord of the office phone nervously. "I'm sorry Oliver. I just wasn't expecting that, you know."

"It's understandable, Kelly," Oliver said. "I shouldn't have been so forward. It's just that I realized I made a huge mistake that day that I left you. I've regretted it all of this time. I know that you'll never give me another chance, but I really just hoped that somehow you would."

"Look, I'm going to cut to the chase here, Oliver," Kelly said, interrupting the man who was pouring out his heart. "I'm in trouble, lots of it. My accountant has been stealing money from me and that's why our company is in this situation in the first place. Today I came to work to find two auditors searching the place. My accountant framed me, stole two and a half million dollars from me, and made it look like I did it with her. I need a damn good lawyer, Oliver, and I don't have any way to afford one. You're the only person I can ask for help. I'll spend one night with you Oliver, whatever it takes."

Silence cut through the line, as Oliver took in Kelly's offer.

"The cost of a lawyer like that couldn't be afforded by one night with you Kelly," he began. "I want a whole weekend with you for that price."

"Deal" replied Kelly solemnly, hanging up the phone.

She wished she hadn't uttered the last words that she had spoken.

Kelly parked in front of the truck stop. She sat in her SUV, nervously waiting for Oliver's arrival. She looked into her rearview mirror, admiring her glistening yellow locks that were blowing in the summer's wind. She may have never wanted to see Oliver Welch ever again, but here she was waiting for him. She had no other choice.

Kelly glanced at the clock, 3:45. Oliver was late by fifteen minutes. Fear began to sink into her chest. What if he decided to not show up? She wouldn't put it past him. Last she remembered of Oliver was him leaving her at the university courtyard five years ago. The two of them were scheduled to have a quiet evening alone together, but when Kelly went to meet him that night, instead she found herself crushed. He told her that she was too young for him to have anything real with and that he thought they both were headed in different directions in their lives. He kissed her on the forehead and left, leaving Kelly standing there all alone in the rain.

Kelly punched the dashboard of her car. Where the hell is he? She screamed out a frustrated growl, clenching her teeth between it. The knock on her window surprised her. Kelly turned around to see Oliver standing outside of the SUV, holding a bouquet of roses. She quickly unrolled her window, a bewildered look upon her face.

"Mad about something?" Oliver asked with a smirk.

"Uh...just my CD player acting up again," Kelly quickly replied, trying to suppress her anger.

"Here, I got these for you," said Oliver, still smiling. "I hope you weren't bothered that I was running a bit late. I wanted to get flowers for you and got stuck in traffic."

Kelly swiftly grabbed the bouquet from Oliver's hand. She questioned the butterflies that were flying around in her stomach. She only agreed to spend a weekend away with Oliver so that she could save her company from going under. Why was she starting to feel enamored by him?

"No, I figured you got caught up with something," she replied. "So where are we headed?"

"The Catskill Mountains," said Oliver, pretending not to notice Kelly's large breasts spilling out of her blouse. "I have a cabin up there. I thought it would be a nice place to get away together, to have some time to talk."

"Yeah. Sounds wonderful," said Kelly, half-heartedly. "You take the lead. I'll follow you."

Oliver flashed one last smile at Kelly and walked toward his car, leaving Kelly wondering why she was starting to lust for him.

The drive to Oliver's cabin took a lot longer than Kelly had expected, but once they reached the destination, Kelly knew why Oliver wanted to spend a weekend with her there. It was beautiful, more gorgeous than anything Kelly had ever seen before. She was so used to the concrete jungle of New York City that she almost forgot a breathtaking world outside of it existed. The cabin looked like those in movies, built entirely by logs. It sat on what seemed like miles of acres full of lush trees and wildflowers. On the long driveway that led to the estate, Kelly could see horses lining its fields. Even though Kelly planned to refuse any romantic advances that Oliver would put on her that weekend, she knew that coming to his estate would be worth her trouble. With everything going on in Kelly's life right now, a little relaxation seemed worth it.

Oliver got outside of his car and walked toward Kelly's. He opened the door and let her out like a true gentleman. The two of them stood outside the car talking.

"So what do you think?" Oliver asked.

"It's absolutely beautiful," said Kelly. "Do you own all of this land?"

"Yes," replied Oliver. "It's my home away from home. I spend much of my time here. Sometimes with business, you just need a place to get away for a while. This is my place."

The two stood in silence, Kelly not knowing what exactly to say.

"How about you look around for a while?" Oliver asked. "I'll take our bags in and get dinner ready for us."

"Sure," replied Kelly, handing Oliver her luggage. "I'll see you in a bit."

Oliver beamed up at Kelly and walked into the cabin, leaving Kelly alone in the wilderness. Kelly stood and thought, remembering how she and Oliver used to talk about getting a place together in the woods one day. Oliver was born in England and spent much of his childhood living in its countryside. He came to the United States to get a taste of the American culture and winded up teaching English at the university

Kelly attended. It was always clear though that the country still breathed in his soul.

Kelly smiled. Oliver hadn't changed very much; he still was attractive, he still was charming, and he still managed to seem like he was stuck to his roots. Whatever was going to happen this weekend, Kelly just hoped he wouldn't leave her alone again, stringing her along on a roller coaster ride that would end in disappointment.

Kelly walked toward the edge of the water and took a seat. She wondered if the manmade lake came with the property or if it was something Oliver had designed in the blueprints. She found herself lost in the serenity of it all: the birds chirping, the breeze flying through the trees, the sound of the bullfrogs. It had seemed like ages since Kelly felt at such peace. Her only hope was that she could control her desires. Seeing Oliver brought back memories she wished she never had, memories that felt like she never forgot. It would be all too easy to fall in love with the man again—his British accent, the dimple that formed in the crease of his smile, his compassion, and his chivalry. Anger flooded through her veins, remembering that the man she was now going to spend a weekend with after all these years had left her and had taken away from her all of the things that she loved.

"Mind if I sit next to you?" asked Oliver, interrupting Kelly's silence, two wineglasses in his hands.

Kelly jumped; he had startled her. She was so dazed in her own reflection that she almost forgot that she had come to the cabin to spend a weekend with Oliver.

"Sure, of course not," Kelly insisted, reaching for a wineglass and pretending not to be bothered.

"I love this lake," Oliver continued. "When I saw that it came with the property, that was when I knew that I had to just get it."

Kelly took a sip of the wine.

"It is beautiful," Kelly admitted. "I almost got lost in just staring into it."

Oliver chuckled and wrapped his arm around Kelly's tense shoulder.

"Dinner is done," he said. "Shall we?"

Kelly sat through dinner listening to the dullness of Oliver's story. As fascinating as his career switch from English professor to owner of Smith & Welch really was, there was something missing. Kelly was only fooling herself by thinking that she was still disgusted by Oliver. He was brilliant and sexy. His deep green eyes pierced right through her. There were moments in which he would lean in and flash his bright, shiny smile at her that made her want to throw their plates of steak off of the table and jump right on top of his meat. Who cared about all of the hurt, pain, and years of mistrust he bestowed upon her? Right now, the moment seemed right and right now rather than her dinner, Kelly was hungry for him.

"So what were the plans that you had in store for us this weekend?" Kelly asked, abruptly interrupting Oliver's recollection of his life since her.

Oliver sat back in his chair and cleared his

throat, taken aback by Kelly's interruption.

"Well, I thought tonight if you were up to it, we could continue having drinks by the lake after dinner, maybe go for a swim," he started. "Then tomorrow I'd love to go horseback riding with you, maybe hike a trail or two."

Kelly leaned across the table, looking at the weakened expression upon Oliver's face.

"You know what I meant Oliver," she said sternly. "What do you plan on getting out of me this weekend? Is it sex?"

"Kelly!" he exclaimed, slamming his wineglass onto the table. "You know that I don't just see you as that."

"Oliver," Kelly continued grimly. "I don't know what you want. You whisk me away to your private estate for the weekend. You say you want to make things up to me for all of the hurt that you've done and here you've just wasted the last hour talking about work. Getting me this lawyer will be worth a lot, even sex I suppose. I just want to know where your thoughts are headed."

Oliver reached across the table, pulling Kelly toward him. He looked into her pale blue eyes and slowly planted his lips onto hers, combing her gorgeous wavy locks away from her face. Kelly passionately kissed him back, licking his lips with her tongue. She was startled by Oliver's hesitation when he broke free of their kiss.

"Kelly, leaving you that night was the worst decision of my life," he said, staring into her eyes. "There hasn't been a day that I haven't thought about you—about what our life would've been if we have stayed together. I've dated other women, women of my age, who could not even begin to compare to you. I don't care about money. I don't care about the lawyer. I'd do that all for you for free. I owe it to you, but I can't stop my lustful desire to feel your kiss and taste your skin once more. What I want Kelly is to be with you. I want to try to make this work. I want to prove to you that I am worth forgiving."

"Oh Oliver," Kelly gasped, reaching her hands around his neck and pulling him in toward her for another kiss. "Take me to the bedroom. Make love to me, Oliver."

Oliver unlocked from Kelly's embrace and stood up, wiping his mouth with a cloth napkin. Kelly stared up at him, wondering if what she had just said was too forward, but Oliver took away all of her fears when he leaned down over her and scooped her right up into his arms. They giggled, as Oliver carried Kelly into the cabin's bedroom and laid her down onto the flannel sheets. He lay next to her, moving her hair away from her face and pressing his lips against hers in order to share another kiss.

"Mmm...Oliver," Kelly moaned, her tongue still entwined with Oliver's. "You taste so right. I'm so glad that you convinced me to spend this weekend with you. All of these years I've yearned to meet another man like you and I never have. Let's make this weekend last. I want to savor every moment of our passion."

Oliver backed out of the kiss, now looking down at Kelly and smiling at her.

"I love you, Kelly Fontanne," he whispered

into her ear. "But I still have a lot of making up to do. Lie down and let me show you just how sorry I am."

Kelly lay like a rag doll on the bed as Oliver slid down her body, licking every inch of it with his tongue. He lowered himself down until he reached Kelly's pussy that was now wet and slid up her dress with his hands. He gently pulled down her lace panties, feeling himself harden with Kelly's sensual giddiness. She was laughing sexily, moaning in between her cheer. Oliver took his hands and used them to spread her swollen pink pussy lips. Upon entering the folds, Oliver beamed in delight, his reaction to the moistness that was already awaiting his mouth. He leaned down, taking a playful bite onto Kelly's puffy clit. Kelly moaned out in ecstasy, using her hands to smash Oliver's face harder into her cunt. This reaction drove Oliver wild, making him lavishly lick up and down Kelly's hot slit. He used a free hand to pull Kelly's tits out of her dress, using his other to ravish his dick. Oliver pulled each nipple through his fingers, one at a time, as he inserted his thick tongue in and out of Kelly's hole with force. Kelly's hips grinded into Oliver's mouth, making him fuck her pussy hole faster and faster.

"Oh my god, Oliver," Kelly screamed. "You're making me cum."

Kelly's hot fluids shot out onto Oliver's lips and tongue. Her body rattled in its own heat and exhaustion. She lay still after her orgasm, legs shaking uncontrollably, locking eyes with Oliver who was happily cleaning his face with his tongue now, licking up every last drop of her cum.

Without warning, Oliver jumped on top of Kelly, roughly inserting his thick cock inside of her. He pulled up Kelly's legs behind his head and rammed his cock in and out of her, hitting her back wall and making her feel like she was going to cum at any instant. Kelly tugged at her nipples, moaning from the sensations that were rippling throughout her body. She moved a free hand down to the area of her pussy, grabbing Oliver's cock as it slammed in and out of her pussy. Oliver moaned, watching the beautiful woman now rub her own clit after naughtily teasing his cock.

"Oh shit," he yelled, his British accent penetrating the air. "I'm going to cum."

"Me too, baby," Kelly moaned in response, feeling the tightness of her pussy muscles clenching at his cock.

The two exploded inside of each other, moaning loudly into the night's air. Oliver fell on top of Kelly, attempting to catch his breath. Kelly watched as each of her pants caused her chest to lift in fall. They breathed together in unison, searching for air.

"That was amazing," Oliver recalled, lifting his body off of Kelly's body and lying beside her. "You truly are an amazing woman."

Kelly smiled and wrapped her arms around Oliver's torso. She fell asleep that night, listening closely to Oliver's heartbeat while she laid her head upon his chest.

CRBO

The smell of bacon cooking wafted throughout the cabin. Kelly came to the conclusion that Oliver was in the kitchen making breakfast as she peeled open her tired eyes. She stretched out in the bed, feeling no desire to leave just yet from its comfort. The soft fabric of the flannel comforter felt like warm silk brushing against her skin. Kelly listened to the sizzle of the meat frying in the other room and the joyous birds singing their happy tune outside of the bedroom window. Compared to the bustle of business in New York City, waking to these sounds seemed like music to Kelly's ears. She smiled, recounting the night she had spent with her old lover. Oliver always knew just the right way to make love to her. If anybody in the world knew how to eat pussy, Oliver would win first prize.

Kelly sat up and stretched out her arms, taking in a sleepy yawn. She could hear the mumble of Oliver's voice speaking to somebody that wasn't there; he must've been on the phone. Kelly felt a curiosity boiling in her stomach. Oliver brought her out here to spend a weekend away from it all; who on Earth was so important that he was talking to them in the middle of nowhere?

Kelly pulled out a robe from one of the bags that she had packed and quickly threw it on. She was determined as hell to find out whom Oliver was talking to. A feeling of guilt struck Kelly as she leaned against the bedroom door, putting her ear against it in order to hear Oliver's conversation. His voice was mumbled, but Kelly could make out a few things—things that made her heart sink.

"We'll have the deal closed up in no time" Kelly heard Oliver say. "Once this weekend is over, Indie Publishing will be part of Smith & Welch. All I have to do is buy their CEO a lawyer and get them out of this funk. Paul is the best damned lawyer in New York City; there's no way that we'll lose and before you know it, Indie Publishing will be under our hold."

Panic struck, as Kelly stumbled away from the door onto the floor. She felt sick to her stomach, knowing that she slept with the man who now sounded like he was deceiving her again. She knew that the catch to the whole deal was that Oliver Welch would parent Indie Publishing, but his tone of voice was unsettling.

All of these years since being crushed by Oliver, Kelly learned how to be independent, to be strong. She didn't take shit from anybody and she got what she wanted. She used men like most women use cosmetics, only needing them when the feeling felt right and washing them off right after. She had no intentions to ever fall in love again—to ever open herself up to a single soul. Going against her instincts and meeting Oliver in New Jersey was a rash last-minute decision that was now becoming a nightmare. Before Kelly even knew that Oliver was the head of Smith & Welch, she knew that she didn't want to merge her company with another. There was too much to lose, too much risk involved, but the company's debt outweighed the cons. Now here she was a week later, not just agreeing to combine with Smith & Welch nor just asking for a hand in help, but sleeping with the CEO and actually believing that he had her best interests in heart. Kelly lay down, crumpled onto the floor with one word ringing in her mind. Fool.

Kelly felt the burn of her tears streaming down her face when Oliver walked into the bedroom, two plates of a fresh-made breakfast in both hands. He searched the bed looking for his sleeping beauty, only to find a mess of the woman on the floor. He studied her body, seeing the tears that were running down her face. Oliver had thought they spent one of the greatest nights of their lives together last night, so why was this woman crying?

"Kell...,"Oliver started. "Is something wrong? Why are you crying?"

Kelly jumped up from her sorrow. She hadn't seen Oliver standing there.

"The deal is off!" she screamed, throwing her clothing into her bags. "I don't know how in the hell I am going to get up from out of the water with this one, but I'll let you know, Oliver Welch, it isn't going to be by the help from you or your company."

Oliver placed the plates onto the bed and rushed over to Kelly in an attempt to stop her.

"Kelly, what the heck happened to you?" Oliver questioned, resting his arm around Kelly's shoulder. "I mean last night was great, magical if you will. I've already told you that I love you, Kelly. I want to help you because I love you. Don't you understand that?"

"Love me?" Kelly accused, brushing off Oliver. "You don't love me! You never loved me! Oliver, it's quite clear to me that the only person you love is yourself. If you even love that. You've lied and deceived me in the past and here you are doing the same in the present. What type of idiot do you take me for?"

Oliver backed away. Kelly was too maddened to convince and he knew when he had to just let a woman go.

"I don't understand what went wrong, Kelly," he said solemnly. "We had an incredible night together. What did I do to change your mind?"

Kelly grabbed her last bag off of the bedroom chair. She turned around and stared blankly at Oliver's shocked expression, hands angrily at her waist.

"Stop thinking that I am a fool, Oliver," Kelly yelled. "I may have been a young woman when we first met each other, but I've grown immensely since then. I've hardened myself against the idea of love, avoiding any opportunity to make myself vulnerable. I allowed you to break open my wall, and for what? To be lied to? To be used? Is that all I am to you, Oliver, a pawn in your sick game? I heard you talking to somebody on the phone earlier, telling him that Indie Publishing was going to be under your control in no time. This whole weekend was a lie, just so you could get your hands on my company. Well, over my dead body you are!"

Oliver stood horrified. He never expected that Kelly would hear his conversation. He had thought that she was sleeping, and now he realized that he was terribly wrong.

"Wait!" Oliver pleaded, chasing Kelly to the front door. "This is all a misunderstanding. That was not what I meant at all. Just hear me out, Kelly!"

Kelly turned from the front door and stared at the desperate man before her. He may have fooled her twice, but there was no way in hell he was ever going to again.

"I'm tired of 'hearing you out.' You are a sham!" Kelly exclaimed firmly.

"Good bye, Oliver. Good riddance for once and for all."

Kelly reached into her glove compartment and pulled out a pack of cigarettes she had been hiding there. She pulled off the cellophane and opened the pack, putting a stale cigarette in between her lips and lighting it. Smoking had always been Kelly's vice before she quit, but under current circumstances, she needed its comfort once again. Chewing gum just wouldn't equate.

Miles had passed since Kelly had left the estate, her lead foot still heavily pressing against the pedal. In the beginning, Kelly had felt like she never wanted to return to the concrete city, but now she wanted to be in its excitement once more. She had never felt so angry.

"God damn it, asshole!" Kelly yelled, looking in her rearview at the driver who was tailgating behind her. "Get off of my ass!"

The car continued, almost touching her bumper, when the driver unrolled his window and began yelling at her.

"Kelly!" he yelled. "Let me talk to you. Please pull over."

"Fuck you!" Kelly screamed in response, throwing the cigarette butt out of the window.

She pushed harder onto the pedal, her speedometer reaching 90 mph. To her surprise, Oliver caught up with her, still closely behind her. Fuck it, Kelly thought as she brought the car to a halt and pulled over to the side of the road. I might as well let him talk to me; otherwise, he's going to follow me to New York or cause me to have an accident.

Kelly leaned against the passenger side of her vehicle, waiting for Oliver to get out of his car. She pulled another cigarette out of its pack and put it between her lips, lighting it up and inhaling its nicotine through its cotton filter. Oliver opened up his car door and walked toward her.

"Kelly, I didn't lie to you," he pleaded. "You've got to believe me. What you heard on the phone was me talking to my business partner. I was just following up with him on our progress. I did not mean to make it seem like I was trying to take over Indie Publishing. Smith knows all about our affair. He knows that I'm not willing to completely take over. I'm sorry that it sounded that way."

Kelly stood in silence, taking another inhale from the cigarette. She breathed out a cloud of smoke in the direction of Oliver's face.

"Oliver, I don't know what to believe," Kelly said. "I've been put through so much by you. Hell, I've been put through a lot with Indie Publishing alone. The accountant that I entrusted betrayed me. You betrayed me all of those years ago. You made it so that I'd never trust another man again. I can't trust you. I can't trust your intentions in my company, let alone me. How could I trust you, Oliver?"

"Marry me," Oliver pleaded, getting down on his knees in front of Kelly.

Kelly stood frozen as she watched Oliver open the velveteen black box and place a ring encrusted with diamonds onto her left finger. She had no response.

"Kelly," Oliver cried. "I really do love you. I never want to lose you ever again. Anything that I've said since our first meeting has been truthful. I want to help you. I want to help Indie Publishing. I want to love you, always and forever. Please marry me."

Kelly opened her mouth, but no words came out.

"Please marry me, Kelly," Oliver begged. "Please say that you'll be my wife."

Tears came crashing onto Kelly's cheeks. All of the hate and pain that once consumed her body was leaving her now.

"I'll be your wife," Kelly managed to squeak out. "I'll be Mrs. Oliver Welch."

Oliver grabbed Kelly by her waist by delight and picked up her frail body into his arms. The two kissed passionately, their tongues heavily exploring each other's mouth. Oliver could feel Kelly's nipples harden underneath her shirt as they pressed against his chest. He could feel his groin aching to feel inside of her.

"I'm taking you to the woods and making love to you right now," he demanded.

Kelly's only response was to giggle, as she kissed him deeply.

"I love you, Kelly Fontanne," Oliver exclaimed while carrying Kelly further into the woods.

"And I love you, Oliver Welch," Kelly replied, staring up into Oliver's eyes.

They came upon a meadow, no buildings in sight. Oliver leaned over and laid Kelly down onto the soft grass. He stood before her undressing, his cock bulging in his boxer briefs. Kelly looked at him with hungry eyes, almost drooling for a taste of his flesh. She sat on her knees, her head reaching his waist, and pulled out his long member. She teased its tip with her tongue, continuing to playfully lick up and down its shaft. Oliver moaned as he watched the beauty take in his throbbing cock into her mouth. She sucked up and down on his cock, teasing the sides of it with her tongue. Precum escaped from Oliver's cock, finally allowing Kelly the chance to taste him.

"Mmm... baby," Kelly moaned. "You taste so good."

"And you," Oliver began. "Are good at tasting it."

Kelly smiled a sultry smile up at Oliver, now jacking off his cock with her hands.

"I have to get inside of you," Oliver begged. "I don't want to waste my orgasm on myself."

Kelly licked the tip of Oliver's cock one last time and laid doggy style onto the grass in anticipation. She could hear Oliver moaning as he slid his fat dick inside of her pussy from behind. The position, Kelly could feel, was making her pussy stretch out to take him in. The pain quickly turned into pleasure as she felt him slam his cock further up her hot cunt. Oliver smacked her ass and rode her wildly, rampaging her pussy with each thrust. Kelly moved her hand to rub her clit in front of her. The pressure of her fingers against the penetration of Oliver's cock made her squirt her orgasm unexpectedly all over his cock. Oliver looked down at the bouncing ass in front of him and noticed that Kelly's cum was left lingering on his dick. Knowing that he made Kelly orgasm was enough for his balls to shoot cum up his shaft. He cried out in pleasure as he let loose his creamy fluids inside of her. Kelly continued to ride his cock until she felt it grown limp. She laid her belly against the grass in exhaustion.

Oliver pulled out of Kelly's pussy and quickly got dressed. His dick twitched inside of his underwear as he admired the naked body of the woman he loved lying on the grass. He vowed to himself that he would never hurt this woman again. Unlike business, love had no price tag and the love that he had shared with Kelly was priceless.

3 BEG FOR YOUR FORGIVENESS

Cold eyes darted across the room. There was Brad Clark standing, huddled around of circle of interested colleagues eating up his every word. Brad could convince these dim wits that nuking a small country would be worth it if it meant gaining the company more profits. These people believed everything that came out of his mouth. They worshiped him and admired his ability to make a sale out of every prospect. Vanessa, on the other hand, didn't.

She lowered her eyes back into her book. This was her lunch break. She had no intentions of listening to the madness that this man was spewing. In fact, she decided to eat lunch at her desk today, originally thinking she'd be able to have a little piece of quiet. She thought by eating lunch at her desk that she would be able to avoid him and his team of followers. Of all days, today she was wrong. Her only escape from the noises now causing her head to want to explode was each page she could indulge further into.

Vanessa crossed her eyes. She was going to need some Tylenol stat. The laughter of Brad's egotism was too much for her to handle. Even though she tried to run away from it in her fantasy collection, she couldn't. Her eyes glanced back to the big circle standing across the room on accident. Locking eyes with Brad, who was now watching her with a disgusted look on his face, was not intentional. Oh, shit! He had seen her.

It was now only going to be a matter of seconds before he'd walk towards her and make her feel like she had no reason to breathe life. Brad made sure of making Vanessa Hudson feel like the smallest person on earth. He didn't care much for the people he couldn't get to buy into him. Vanessa Hudson was just a parasite he wished he could eradicate from his existence or even the Earth, for that matter.

Vanessa fiddled around with the plastic bottle of pills, trying to make herself look busy. She didn't want an opportunity for her eyes to look over towards him. She looked down, hearing the footsteps of his heavy walk nearing towards her. She'd just try to ignore him, she thought. Maybe if she seemed busy, he would find her too dull at the moment to harass. Sadly today, like most days, Vanessa's assumptions were wrong.

"Hey Ness," she heard his voice thunder in the now silent room. "Did you hear about the contract I got with W.D. & Sons?"

Vanessa didn't look up from the pills she was pretending not to be able to open. If she ignored him, would he go away?

"Yes, I heard," Vanessa responded coldly, after what seemed like hours of silence stood before them. "Of course, I heard you, Brad; I believe the whole office knows the story now."

Brad chuckled that of a king laughing at the peasants fighting for bread in the streets.

"You know, Ness...," he started. "You never seem interested in the contracts that I get. As the Financial Controller, you should make yourself interested in the outcomes of your best Sales Director."

He paused, staring down at the only woman he had met who showed no interest in him.

"But who am I kidding?" he continued with another laugh. "You're more interested in reading fantasy books than you are living in the real world. I have no idea why they keep you here. You're pathetic."

The blood began to boil in Vanessa's veins.

"I'm pathetic?" she responded sharply, looking into the evil that could be seen in Brad Clark's eyes. "You're the most arrogant, conceited, egotistical, self-centered, pompous excuse for a man that I have ever had the opportunity to meet. I'm sorry Brad that I'm not one of these girls at the office who wants to suck your cock for a taste of your feeble fucking existence. You may be one of the best Sales Directors on our team, but don't forget who the Financial Controller is here, okay? Now if you'll excuse me, I have fifteen minutes left of my lunch and I'm going to spend it in quiet, away from you."

Brad stood over her desk in disbelief. Vanessa had never spoken such harsh words towards him. Whenever he'd try to excite her with anger, he never seemed able to win. She'd normally just ignore him or roll her eyes. As much as he always hoped she'd fight back, he had never expected her to call him out in this sort of way. No woman ever turned down Brad Clark, and although he always knew she showed him no interest, he never expected the woman to completely despise him.

He laughed, breaking the thick air between them.

"Okay, Ms. Financial Controller" he said, backing away from her desk. "Go back to reading about dragons and fairies. Some of us actually have lives to live."

Vanessa's eyes didn't move. She now had her head buried into the book, feeling the rush of euphoria running throughout her body. She finally told Brad to fuck off. It took a lot of guts, but she did it. Nothing that he could say to her now could faze her.

"See you at the Christmas party tonight," he said with a click sounding from between his teeth.

He saluted her and walked out the door.

Fuck!

Vanessa completely forgot about the Christmas party tonight. Industrial Solutions was up to their ears with business this year, thanks to Brad, and she had been so busy crunching numbers for tax purposes that she forgot about the company's yearly party. She thought about avoiding it. She could just claim that it slipped her mind, but Vanessa knew better than that. Rick Dobbs, of course, would be making his appearance tonight, and being that he was the head honcho of the company, he expected to see everyone there, especially his Financial Controller. Besides, it was always worth it to show up. The annual Christmas party meant the annual Christmas bonus. With the figures they brought in this year, it would be well worth the dry four hours Vanessa would have to suffer through.

She walked into her apartment feeling completely empowered. Telling off Brad meant the confidence of a lifetime for Vanessa and she had it now. The profits earned this year would surely mean at least an extra five grand in her pocket tonight also, so no matter how unprepared she was for the event, she was going to make it work. The only problem was what to wear.

Vanessa opened up the folded closet doors. The apparel that lay before her was so lifeless, so drub. Nothing but solid colored pieces and sheathe dress after sheathe dress. Vanessa began to feel her newly found confidence slither away. She wanted to look amazing tonight, not like some drab thirty-year-old woman who let herself go. She started to walk towards her bed so she could lie down and sulk when a thought popped into her head; the black tube dress that would surely make her look the way she felt. It lay listless in the back of her closet on its hanger. She had never even worn it she realized, as she pulled the price tags off. Originally, she bought it for the date night she was planning to have with Marcus. That was the night he stood her up and left the message on her answering machine that it was over between them. That was the night when Vanessa's confidence finally went flying out the door.

Never mind the bad memories, she thought. Tonight was going to be different. Tonight she was going to show Brad and everyone else at Industrial Solutions that she was a firecracker of a woman who they should handle with care. Tonight was going to be different. Vanessa Hudson was going to prove everyone that she was a force to be reckoned with.

Two bubbly ass cheeks bounced up and down on a stiffened shaft. Hands slapped the ass, causing an aftermath of jiggles that resembled that of snow falling due to an avalanche. The woman screamed out in ecstasy as she exploded her white fluids all over the hardened cock. Two hands lifted the ass of the now lifeless woman up and down on the shaft. The woman continued to moan as she felt her orgasm completing its eruption throughout her body. The man underneath her moaned out in pleasure as he began to feel his cock stiffen even harder as his balls released its juices inside the woman's cunt. Two bodies lie comatose on top of each other, each of the owners smiling in their own bliss.

"You have to leave," the man said coldly, while lifting the woman's spent body off of him. "You know where the door is."

The woman sat up and stared at the man angrily. How could he just have sex with her and make her leave? She thought this man had some sort of feelings for her, and now here he was making her feel used and abused.

"What the fuck Brad?" the woman asked a scornful look on her face. "How are you just going to have sex with me and then make me leave like I'm some piece of trash?"

Brad laughed.

"I wouldn't say you're trash, Shirley" he began. "God, you're at least a recyclable."

"A recyclable?" asked the woman, who was now screaming. "You're the biggest asshole I have ever met!"

Brad threw Shirley's clothes at her from across the room and pointed towards the door.

"You know where the door is," he said, repeating himself. "Find your way out."

He chuckled to himself at the reflection of the angry woman leaving his apartment. These dumb whores, he thought to himself. They always thought they were the one. They always wanted more. Couldn't they tell that Brad Clark only cared about Brad Clark? There was never going to be a woman to domesticate him and pull him by a leash. Brad Clark was invincible.

Well almost. Thoughts flooded his mind about Vanessa, as he got ready for the party. She was the only person he had met who was able to block him with a shield of steel. No matter what he said or did, he couldn't get her admiration, not even for a second. Most of the women that he took home or even encountered eventually realized he was a complete prick, but it took a lot of work to make them actually see it. Vanessa, on the other hand, knew right from the moment he walked into Industrial Solutions. Vanessa has always been cold to him.

Rather than get mad at the fact that Vanessa wouldn't respond to him, he just made in his mind that he disliked her. He saw her as timid, shy, useless, and weird. It was much easier that way than try to impress a woman who wouldn't respond. He had the whole company looking up at him with curious eyes and admiration, so what if one of the thousand employees wouldn't buy into him? Normally, he probably wouldn't have even been so cruel to Shirley, but he had to shake Vanessa's confrontation off. She really pissed him off by attacking him; no one had ever judged his character the way she did.

He tried to push the thoughts of Vanessa far back into his mind. It was bad enough he had to see the hag of a woman at the Christmas party tonight, at least he could make himself look good for everybody else there that would worship him. He put on his cufflinks and looked into the mirror. Damn, he was going to look good tonight. There was no way Vanessa could affect him.

The ballroom was crowded, full of who's who's and noxious chatter. Brad walked confidently across the floor to a circle of men sharply dressed in suits. He felt comfortable in his skin as he made way through these men. All of them idolized him.

They shared small talk on profits. Each man listened intently as Brad filled in the few who hadn't heard earlier about him winning the contract with W.D. & Sons. A few of the men interrupted his boast, as they looked towards the entrance of the room and started whistling.

"Damn!" the man in the blue suit interrupted. "Have you ever seen her look so hot before?"

"Holy Fuck!" responded the man in the gray suit. "She always looks so plain at the office, who would've guessed that she could look like a fox?"

Brad was annoyed that his recount of the contract was being interrupted by the horniness of the men standing around him. Women to him we're nothing more than a source of self-satisfaction. This was a business party, for Christ sakes. He turned around and saw Vanessa standing near the entrance talking with the secretary from the fourteenth floor. Blue and gray suit were right. Vanessa did look damn good tonight.

His mouth stood ajar, as he watched her dark blonde curls bounce with each laugh. Her breasts looked luscious, so perfectly hidden beneath the black tube dress. In all of his years working with Vanessa, Brad never realized how long and sexy her legs were; but with the shortness of her dress and the black stiletto's that raised her figure two inches higher off the ground, he realized it tonight. Vanessa Hudson didn't just look hot, she was absolutely stunning.

Guilt came as a force in the back of Brad's throat, neatly wrapped as a big, thick ball that he was practically choking on. All of these years Vanessa just was a bad taste in his mouth, but tonight he regretted every moment that he had felt that way. She really was a gorgeous beauty and when he actually thought about it, she was extremely intelligent. Unlike all of the other women in the office, or even men, Vanessa had a brain. Industrial Solutions was really making their money off of her because they really couldn't afford what she was worth.

The men carried on with their conversation, Brad really trying to be a part of it, but he couldn't get the thought of Vanessa standing there, gorgeously placed near the entrance out of his mind. Maybe he should apologize for all of the ignorance he had directed at her. After all, it would soon be a new year, and maybe he could make a fresh start. He really didn't want to continue working with someone who despised him. Tonight, he decided, he was going to make it up to her.

"I'll see you guys around," he said to the group of men, interrupting gray suits story.

With that, he made a quick escape heading towards Vanessa's direction.

Vanessa needed a drink.

She was glad to see Jean as soon as she entered the room, as Jean was truly the only good friend she thought she had at Industrial Solutions. Seeing Frank, Jean's husband, on the other hand was truly a different story though. He was a mockery of a man, almost as egocentric as Brad Clark, except without the good looks; listening to his boring small talk and watching his belly fat jiggle with each laugh was enough to make Vanessa want to puke. As much as Vanessa feared being left there to stand alone, she truly was delighted when Frank announced he and his wife were going to excuse themselves to talk with Rick Dobbs. She stood there aimlessly afterwards, considering whether she should go get a drink at the open bar or chat up other fellow employees first. She didn't want to seem rude tonight. Vanessa was done being the timid, shy coworker. She decided a drink would ease her before speaking with everyone tonight and began to make her way towards the bar when she saw Brad Clark headed towards her direction, a sly smile on his face. Oh god, she thought, time to put her game face on.

"Hi Vanessa," Brad began, as he finally made way towards Vanessa. "Enjoying the party so far?"

"Brad, quit the small talk," responded Vanessa harshly. "I didn't come to this party tonight to be annoyed by you."

"Look Ness, about that," he started.

"About what?" Vanessa replied. "About the fact that I finally gave you a piece of my mind earlier? Look, Brad, I'm sick and tired of you harassing me every single day at work. Can't you just understand that I don't like you and leave me alone?"

Brad stood still for a moment. She was still mad at him.

"Ness," he spoke out, after a moment of silence. "Look, I didn't come over here to bother you. I actually came over to apologize about earlier. Well, to apologize about everything really."

Vanessa laughed out loud to herself.

"You apologize?" she accused, pointing her finger in his face. "Brad Clark doesn't apologize. What do you have up your sleeve?"

"I'm being sincere," he pleaded. "I really am Nessa. I know I've been an asshole to you since day one and I'm sorry about that. What you said about me earlier really hit home. I am pretty egotistical. I guess I just expect everyone to respond to me the way everyone else does. You, Vanessa, have proved me wrong though. I think I've just been ignorant to you because you're not a goddamned sheep like everyone else. I truly am sorry for my actions. I've been thinking, and with a New Year right around the corner, I'd rather have you on my side than against me. We could accomplish great things if we worked together."

Vanessa stood and thought for a minute. Was Brad really being truthful? This was a man who was once a snake, a man that seemed to not shelter a soul within his body. How on Earth would Vanessa be able to trust him? One thing he said, though, did strike a chord; they could accomplish great things if they worked together in the company rather than how they were currently working against each other.

"Alright Brad," Vanessa said coyly. "If you want me on your side, how about we grab a drink at the bar together as a start?

"Sounds wonderful," said Brad with a big smile upon his face. "After you, madame."

Vanessa wasn't quite sure how many gin and tonics she had gulped down, but she was starting to feel uncomfortable about the emotions and hormones that were surging throughout her body. Brad, for the first time, was starting to look irresistible to her. She had always known Brad was a good-looking man, whether she chose to appreciate it or not, but now each smile was starting to make her feel wet down below. He was simply sexy and Vanessa realized that she hadn't been touched by a man for over a year now. Just talking to Brad was becoming too much to handle.

Rick Dobbs stood at the podium talking about the profits and companies they had gained throughout the year and his expectations for 2013. Brad and Vanessa both rolled their eyes at each other while viewing the stout man from across the room from the bar. This was the company Christmas party, not a business meeting. It was obvious that Rick Dobbs, Industrial Solutions extraordinaire, had way too much to drink.

"How about we get out of here for a while?" Brad asked, interrupting their silence that was spent on looking at the drunken CEO.

"To where?" Vanessa asked him suspiciously.

Hell, it didn't matter at this point. She wanted out of here, as much as he seemed to.

"To the courtyard," Brad instructed. "It's beautiful there and we could bring some drinks to go. Rick Dobbs is so trashed, he won't even notice."

"Two gin and tonics to go," Vanessa advised the bartender.

Brad was right. The courtyard was beautiful and with nobody else there but her and Brad, it was quite peaceful in comparison to the mess that filled the ballroom. She found herself actually liking Brad. He wasn't being the egotistical maniac that he was inside the office; he actually was proving to her that he was a decent human being. They talked about college and Brad's decision to go from graphic designer to Sales Director at Industrial Solutions. It was a hard decision for him at first, and Brad confided in Vanessa that he carried narcissism at Industrial Solutions because he was only hired as a temporary employee at first. He used his ego to keep his job; he just forgot to let it go once hired on full time.

Vanessa looked into his sparkling hazel eyes. There was a candor that she had never seen before. It may have been all the gin and tonics that she had guzzled down in the last hour, but she leaned in and kissed him. To her surprise, he kissed her back, pulling her in close to him. They locked lips, Vanessa's tongue swirling hard against his. Their passion began to heat up and the two began panting heavily. Brad slowly pushed her back away from him.

"I know this is kind of forward of me, Vanessa," he began. "But would you be interested in ditching this party and finishing up for a nightcap at my place instead?"

Vanessa stood up.

"Let's go."

Brad's loft was everything that Vanessa would've expected. It was luxurious, filled with only the finest things money could afford. She looked at the gorgeous bed covered in blue satin sheets that sat underneath the spiral staircase. This was going to be the place where Brad Clark would make love to her, she decided.

"Would you like a glass of bubbly?" he asked Vanessa.

"That would be absolutely wonderful," she replied.

Brad excused himself and headed towards his kitchen, pouring two glasses of champagne into crystal glasses. Vanessa, who was already feeling quite drunk, lay on the satin sheets and watched the ceiling spin above her head.

She never would've guessed that she'd ever find herself on the bed of Brad Clark.

The glasses stood still on the wicker side table, as Brad and Vanessa passionately unraveled each other's clothes. Brad couldn't help but to sit on the bed and just stare at Vanessa's beautiful body afterwards. She lay perfectly on top of his satin sheets, her breasts lying subtlety on top of her pristine sculpted abdomen. He loved the way the fullness of her hips looked between the thin, black, laced thong. Vanessa was a true goddess. He couldn't believe he never appreciated it before.

Brad sat beside her, teasing her pussy by rubbing it through the outside of the thong. She moaned in pleasure, watching his muscular hands stroking it. She was already wet from earlier in the night when they were just talking at the bar; now her panties were soaked.

Brad gently took the panties down her legs, exposing the small, perfectly trimmed pussy that sat in front of him. He spread her legs while leaning down and inserted his tongue onto her clit. He swirled his tongue in a circle, growing hard with each moan that escaped her lips.

He felt heat rushing down from his chest into his manhood. He wanted to feel Vanessa cum all over his mouth. She tasted so wonderful; he wanted her full taste, not just a few licks. He dragged his heavy tongue down her slit and inserted it in and out of her hole as if it were his dick. She was driving him wild; the idea of her cumming all over him was making pre-cum form at the tip of his cock. While shoving his tongue in and out of her pussy, he used a free hand to gently rub her clit. Her cum came rushing down onto his tongue like a waterfall, covering it with all of her splendor. Her hips shook uncontrollably as he pulled his mouth out from between her and licked her juices off of his lips.

"You're so beautiful, Vanessa," he whispered into her ear, crouching on top of her.

His muscles glistened with sweat, as he inserted his manhood inside of her vagina. The length of his dick was average in size, but its girth made up for it. His dick filled her pussy with force, making her scream in pleasurable agony. Vanessa moved her hips and spread her legs, lifting them up in a V shape around his body. He slammed in and out of her, watching her tits happily bounce up and down with each motion. Vanessa took her hand and forcefully rubbed her swollen clit, making her muscles clench harder around his thick cock. She felt herself cum onto his dick, an orgasm so intense that her body bolted up and down with its release. Brad released himself into her slippery hole, ejaculating so much that his cum was dripping down her thighs before he could even finish.

Drenched in a pool of sweat, Brad lifted himself off of her inanimate body. She lay there, still beautiful, still resembling the goddess he had envisioned earlier. He walked towards a closet and pulled out a towel, which he used to carefully wipe the fluids of their lovemaking off of himself and then her. He lay down next to her and wrapped his arms around her thin waist.

"Thank you, Vanessa," he whispered into her ear. "That was amazing!"

Vanessa didn't answer. She had already fallen asleep.

The sun shined brightly into the windows of Brad's loft, stinging the eyes of a very drowsy Vanessa who had just awakened from her drunken slumber. She glanced over towards the empty spot next to her only to find a crumbled satin sheet that had taken Brad's place from last night. She sighed, pressing her head firmly into the pillow and pulling the blue comforter up over her eyes. For a woman who once despised Brad Clark, Vanessa desperately wanted to kiss him passionately this morning, yet he was nowhere to be found. She was still way too comatose to get off her ass this morning and find him. "Just how many gin and tonics did I drink exactly?" she thought.

Vanessa lay like a corpse on top of the satin sheets; her head wanting to explode from the pounding that was being unleashed inside of it. She felt as if she had been lying there frozen stiff for an eternity before she heard Brad's heavy steps walking towards the bed. Her face lit up with a smile underneath the covers. Finally, she was going to be able to thank him for the hot experience he had shared with her last night. Before unraveling the blanket from her face, she let out a silent chuckle, laughing at the idea that she had fallen for Brad Clark, the man she used to hate.

"Ness, are you up?" Brad questioned, as he reached the bed.

Vanessa quickly pulled the cover off of her body and smiled up at him.

"Yeah, I don't feel very alive though," she responded with a smirk.

"Well that's completely uncool and all...," Brad began to say, after he stood in silence for a few seconds trying to figure out what he was going to exactly tell her. "But I need you to go, Vanessa. Like right now, if that's possible."

The heat of anger began to rise throughout Vanessa's half-dead body as she began to sit up. She may have been drunk last night, but she thought that they had a great time together. She sat in silence for a moment pondering whether or not she blacked out at any point during the night. Did she say something stupid? Did she do something completely out of character that would've made Brad to want her to go away?

As she sat there in Brad's bed, watching the scenes of the night flash before her very eyes, all she could think of was the last words she remembered Brad whispering into her ear. She had lain there half-asleep next to him, but she swore that she had heard him thank her and tell her that their sex was amazing.

"Uh... Did I do something, Brad?" she asked, still wearing a shocked expression on her face. "I mean last night was great from what I can remember. One of the...I mean the only good time we ever had together."

"Yea...well..." Brad stammered, looking at his feet on the floor rather than Vanessa's face. "It was alright. I mean you were drunk and everything...look Vanessa can you please just leave? I don't really want to argue about this. Last night was a complete mistake."

Vanessa jumped out of bed and was already halfway dressed by the time Brad finished his sentence. She couldn't believe the nerve of this guy. Of course, she never expected to forgive Brad last night let alone have sex with him, but she woke up this morning feeling different. Hell, she even thought they had a connection.

"Yeah, a big mistake alright!" Vanessa screamed at him, already halfway out the door of the apartment. "Last night was the biggest mistake of my life. You played me, Brad Clark. You made me actually believe that you were sincere about wanting to have a better work relationship. You made me fall for you by using your charm and my intoxicated judgment. Well you know what, Brad? You win! You fucking win! You wanted me to be like everyone else at the office. You wanted me to like you, to look up to you, to find some sort of value in you. You convinced me into believing in you and you convinced me to have sex with you. Well your charm might have worked last night when I was drunk, but it sure as hell won't ever work again. I'm done with you and I'm done having to deal with you at Industrial Solutions. Fuck you Brad Clark. I hope you die!"

Vanessa finished her last words halfway down the hall of the apartment. I hope you die, still ringing in Brad's ears as he slammed the door in front of him. She'll get over it.

Vanessa felt her lungs almost collapse when she finally realized that she had been running for at least ten blocks now. She came to a complete stop, her lungs gasping for air. The nerve of that man.

Her heart was beating wildly in her chest, making her have to lean against the building beside her just in case she'd pass out. Waking up in Brad's bed that morning felt so right, even with how hungover she felt, she woke up with a desire to taste the flavor of his skin once more; but now she felt dirty. He had used her that night and made her out to look like a complete fool. What kind of sick mind did Brad Clark have to find pleasure in humiliating her? Perhaps she struck a nerve with him at the office earlier that day when she finally gave him a piece of her mind, but he used her for sex to get back at her? This was sick, the whole thing was sick.

Vanessa felt for her cell phone in the back pocket of her jeans. She really needed someone to talk to right now. She felt so disgusting, so filthy. She never even had a one-night stand before, let alone with a man she originally hated, a man who deceived her and used her for sex. If anyone could help her calm down and come to right now, it would be

Kathy. Kathy always was her shoulder to lean on, her person to cry to. She never judged Vanessa for what she did, and she always seemed to make her feel better. Kathy had the best advice in the world as far as Vanessa was concerned, and she desperately needed to talk to her right now.

"Hello?" Kathy finally answered, after what seemed like a million rings.

"Kath..."Vanessa began, tears flooding her cheeks so hard that she almost couldn't move her mouth to talk. "Kathy, I need to talk to you. Do you have a minute?"

"Oh my God, Ness..." exclaimed Kathy on the other line. "What's wrong? What happened? You sound awful!"

"Ka...Ka...Kathy," Vanessa stammered, still fighting for the words to come out. "I've been used. I've been used by a guy at work. I don't know what to do."

"Were you raped?" Kathy demanded. "Are you okay, Nessa? I'm worried for you."

"No...It wasn't rape," Vanessa responded, answering to Kathy's concerns. "I consented to the whole thing. I just didn't expect him to use me the way he did. He's a sick man, Kathy, a terrible man. I don't know why I believed him. I don't know why I fell for his game."

Vanessa felt relief flood over her body that was still leaning against the wall of the building. Kathy's voice was always so soothing, so kind. She listened to the encounter Vanessa had had with Brad the night before, and even though she had already been well informed for some time now that Vanessa despised the man, she didn't judge her. She was so sick and tired of watching her best friend go from one bad relationship to the next. Marcus was bad enough to see her go through, but now this? She was always Vanessa's friend, her main ally. Brad's behavior was simply unacceptable.

"Vanessa, come to Washington for a while. Quit that damned job at Industrial Solutions. I know you like your career, but you can do the same thing for my company, and I even have a spare bedroom you can stay in for a while until you'd get back onto your feet. Sometimes you have to make a tough decision, if it means finding your happiness.

"You know what, Kathy?" Vanessa responded. "You're right. I deserve to find my happiness again. I'll put in my two weeks' notice on Monday."

"That's my girl," the voice of Kathy's voice echoed on the other line.

Rick Dobbs resembled that of a statue sitting upright in his chair. Brad had no idea why he was called into his office, but after the weekend he had, he was pretty sure things couldn't get any worse. He sat nervously in the seat across from his boss, fiddling with the buttons on his suit coat.

"Brad, do you know why I called you into my office today?" Rick questioned him sternly, piercing his eyes with a look that resembled that of a man who was about to eat him alive.

"Uh..." Brad began. "I actually was

wondering that, sir."

Rick leaned back into his office chair and turned it around to view the city's landscape that sat outside the tall office window. He let out a big sigh, placing his hands together and leaning into their tips with his head. The two people sitting across a desk from each other sat in silence, for a very long time.

"Vanessa is leaving in two weeks," Rick finally said, slicing the stale air like a knife. "I'm sure you're well aware of that though."

Brad sunk into the leather of the chair. He actually hadn't been well aware that Vanessa was leaving. Well, besides when she told him that she was done working with him at Industrial Solutions when she ran out of his apartment screaming. He never really expected that she'd put in her two weeks' notice, at least not so soon, not, that following Monday.

Brad shook his head.

"I actually wasn't aware of that, sir," he said dimly.

Silence stood still in the room. Rick Dobbs turned his chair and now faced Brad.

"You know, Mr. Clark, I find it kind of funny that you know nothing about this," he began. "Awfully funny being that you and Ms. Hudson came up missing this past Friday at the Christmas party, then today she comes in and puts in her two-week notice. Furthermore, Mr. Clark, since this fine morning when Ms. Hudson came in and spoke with me, I began to hear rumors of you two around this office; rumors that you have been harassing my Financial Controller for a long time now."

Brad sat back further into the leather of the chair. He could hear the echo of the huge gulp he had taken with his throat now running through his ears. What exactly did Mr. Dobbs know about his and Vanessa's relationship? Did she tell everybody around the office about what they did with each other that night after the Christmas party? Brad sat for a moment, looking down at his hands.

"Well, Mr. Dobbs," he started. "We didn't exactly see eye to eye all of the time. There were a few spouts, an argument here and there."

"An argument? I see..." Mr. Dobbs responded, now getting up from his chair and pouring himself a glass of spirits. "Well what you may not know, Mr. Clark, is that your inability to get along with Ms. Hudson is ruining MY FUCKING BUSINESS!!!"

"But sir..." Brad pleaded.

"Do not sir me!" Rick Dobbs exploded. "Do not ever interrupt me while I am speaking! You, Brad Clark, are lucky that today is your lucky day and that your ass is not getting canned instead! Vanessa Hudson was one of the best things that ever happened to this company and now she is leaving. She is not leaving because she dislikes this company or because she dislikes her career, she is leaving because she dislikes you and this is your entire fucking fault!"

"But sir..."Brad stammered.

Rick Dobbs held his hand out to silence Brad. He took a long sip from his whiskey glass, finishing the drink, and then slamming the glass onto a table. Brad was certain that he had never seen the man so angry in his entire career while working at Industrial Solutions. He realized that there was no good in trying to convince Rick Dobbs that he wasn't at fault for Vanessa leaving the company, being that he knew deep down inside that Friday's incident was the exact reason why she was. He felt downright awful and waited in silence, slumped down into the chair, feeling like an ant in Mr. Dobbs eyes. He not only hurt his career, he hurt Vanessa and now she was leaving because of him.

"Let's get a few things straight," said Rick. "You sir, are DISPOSABLE! I can find any punk ass kid to be my Sales Consultant any day of the week. All I have to do is walk the streets and find the most egotistical piece of shit, like yourself, to replace you. Vanessa...well, Vanessa was special. She was personable, she had an enormous amount of skill, an exception in the realm of innovative ideas, and I liked her. She was easy to please and did her job well. Frankly, she deserved more than what we could afford to pay her, but she did her job anyway and she did it with a smile on her face."

"What I want you to do, Mr. Clark, if you still want your position here at Industrial Solutions that is," he continued, "is to find Vanessa and make up for whatever you said or did to her. And I'm not just saying that you go and try to apologize to her. You take her out to dinner, you buy her some flowers, you buy her a $1500 Prada purse, and you do whatever it takes to win her back. Do you understand me, Mr. Clark? You get Vanessa Hudson to keep her job with us at Industrial Solutions and if you don't sir, you will be fired!"

Brad gulped and began to stand up nervously.

"Yes...s...s...sir..." he began. "I'll do whatever it takes."

Rick Dobbs shot an evil smile towards Brad's direction.

"You are excused, Brad," he said. "You have one week."

"One week, got it!" exclaimed Brad, as he walked out the door.

Brad leaned against the now closed door and sulked. How in the world was he going to get Vanessa to stay at Industrial Solutions? Better yet, how was he going to tell her the truth? The truth that he truly had fallen in love with her after all of these years and ruined it because he was too afraid of commitment?

Brad laid on the satin sheets of his bed staring up the high ceiling in front of him. Brad had spent so many years avoiding his emotions, but this weekend and now today had proven to him that when you hide your emotions, they eventually find you. He stretched out his arms and legs across the bed, letting out a loud moan. This was going to be tough. He had to get Vanessa back to work in order to save his career working for

Mr. Dobbs. He had to get Vanessa back because he was madly in love with her.

Brad turned around and smashed his face into the pillow. He could still smell the faint smell of Vanessa's apple blossom shampoo on his pillowcase. She smelled so wonderful that night. He smiled thinking of the way they made love to each other. How wonderful it could've been if he wouldn't have been such a pansy, so afraid of releasing the emotions he had been hiding from her all of these years. He originally woke that morning after, placing his arms around Vanessa and holding her thin waist. He planned in his mind that they would go out and have breakfast together once she awoke. He planned to tell her that he has been suppressing his feelings for her all of these years and that he only pestered her because he liked her; getting any reaction from her was better than no reaction at all, at least that's what he thought.

In the beginning, Brad tried to flirt with her. He had tried almost everything in his book of tricks, but she showed no interest in him whatsoever. All of the other women in the office swooned over his good looks, all of them almost begging to get on their knees and have a taste of his dick, but Vanessa wasn't one of them. She always seemed too busy, too wrapped up in a book or her work to even notice him standing there. Once his reputation built up at Industrial Solutions, so did Brad's confidence in himself. He had all of the money in the world to show a woman a good enough time - great looks, fast cars, and nice things. Women were practically lining up at his doorstep, but it got boring. Having lifeless sex with woman after woman turned the whole act into something drearily mundane. Big tits, small tits, thick ass, and no ass, it was all turning into the same thing for Brad. With a loft apartment and the six-figure salary that could afford a new yacht or Porsche every year, materialism had grown dull too. Brad felt like he had conquered everything there was for a man to conquer, except Vanessa.

Her lack of interest turned Brad's irritation into disdain. He hated Vanessa for everything she was; her beauty that she hid behind drab clothes, her spunk that she hid behind books and paperwork, her power that she hid behind timidness, and her intelligence that she chose to rarely show. He hated how she'd just sit there behind her desk, avoiding an opportunity to converse with anyone at the office. He hated that she'd avoid the opportunity to converse with him, mostly. Everybody else looked up to Brad Clark as if he was a god, but not Vanessa, and that pissed him off the most. She had too much self-discipline.

Brad started bothering Vanessa as merely a way to get some excitement out of her. He figured that if he could make her dislike him every day, at least he would be in her mind some way or another. He thought over time he'd be able to break her in and that he'd be able to get her to respond to him in a pleasant way. He really hated to even have to put her down in this manner, but seeing the frown on his face became pleasurable in some way. If he couldn't have her, he'd slowly destroy her. His ego was becoming bigger than he was.

Brad lay in bed, his face still down in the pillow. Why did he make her leave? He finally had won her over and he was too scared to pursue her. What a mockery he had made of himself! The all-powerful, arrogant, self-centered Brad Clark had chosen his desire to be in control of everything rather than to fall in love with the woman who made him become this monster because she denied him her affection.

Brad sprang out of bed.

"Fuck!" he muttered to himself. "I have to win Vanessa back! Not for the company, but for me. I love this woman."

Vanessa was in her apartment packing her boxes for the move to Washington. Tears started to form in her eyes when she walked past her dining room and looked out its bay view window. She really loved this place. The whole idea of leaving it was breaking her heart, but she couldn't continue working at the same company as a man who had torn her heart into a million little pieces.

She walked past the mirror in the hallway and laughed at her reflection. God, she looked terrible today. She had barely combed her hair that day and it was almost impossible to get dressed. She stared at the dull khaki suit she was wearing. She looked like an old rag. "I'm in for the night," she said to herself. "Pajamas and a nice cup of tea are in order."

Vanessa was walking downstairs in her purple kimono bathrobe when the doorbell rang. She figured it might've been Kathy to come and check on her, so she rushed down the stairs to open the door. Kathy would defiantly be okay seeing her look reckless in a bathrobe with untamed hair. Kathy, again, was a woman with no judgments. Without even looking out of her peephole, she quickly opened the door to find Brad standing there with a vase of roses in his hands.

"What the hell do you want?" She asked angrily, trying to hide the kimono inspired robe behind the door.

"Vanessa..." Brad stammered. "I need...I need...to talk to you."

"There is nothing to talk about Brad," she said, now yelling. "I'm done with you and I'm done with Industrial Solutions. It's about time that I find my own happiness in this life."

Vanessa went to slam the door in Brad's face, but Brad counteracted the motion by blocking the door and its hinges with his hand.

"Look...Ness..." he pleaded, looking at the bewildered expression on her face. "Can we please just talk? You're going to leave the company anyway. I won't ever see you again. Just hear me out, okay? Please?"

Vanessa stood still, noticing the sincerity in Brad's facial expressions. She questioned if she should even give him the opportunity to hear him out being that he seemed so sincere at the Christmas party that night and proved otherwise that following morning. One thing he was right about though, she wouldn't be seeing Brad Clark ever again, and so what difference would it make if she talked to him again? Heck, she might even have one last opportunity to tell him off.

"Ok Brad, come in," she said, leading him into her living room with the direction her finger was pointing towards. "I'll warn you that I'm half dressed. I was planning on spending the night in and relaxing without company."

Although the silk robe had only showcased Vanessa's body in a subtle way, Brad could not help noticing how sexy she looked wearing it – her long, lean legs exposed underneath it, the way it perfectly hugged her ample breasts. Her tits we're almost begging to be unleashed from the fabric, to have Brad's tongue flicking against their bare skin. He could feel the flesh of his cock begin to stiffen in his pants but had to quickly remind himself that he was coming to see Vanessa so he could win her back, not to fuck her again.

"These are for you," Brad said to Vanessa, handing her the roses he had picked up for her.

"They're nice and all Brad..." quickly replied Vanessa, grabbing the roses and sitting down the vase onto her coffee table. "But why the fuck are you here? I mean, seriously?"

"Look Ness..." Brad began, hesitantly. "I've done some thinking and I've realized that the night we shared was the biggest mistake of my life. Not because we had sex, but because I had let you go. You see, Vanessa, I've liked you ever since I started working at Industrial

Solutions and I have just have been too much of a pussy to tell you. In the beginning, I tried to get your attention, but you just never seemed interested in me. Every other woman on the planet wanted me, besides the one woman that I wanted. I guess I just let my arrogance destroy me. I let it dictate who I was and I let it overcome the one thing I really wanted. I asked you to leave that day not because I thought what we shared was a mistake, but because I didn't know how to tell you my true feelings. I love you, Vanessa. You are the most beautiful, passionate, charming, and caring person that I know. I want you to reconsider your decision to move to Washington. If you don't want to stay at Industrial Solutions that's fine, but please allow me a chance to prove to you just how much I love you."

Vanessa stared at Brad in silence. Was what he said really true? He had lied to her before, was this just another game of his to lie to her again? What would be the purpose of it though? Was there really anything he could gain out of this?

Vanessa had to admit what he had just said was one of the sweetest things a man had ever told her. Vanessa had to admit that the words that had just been spewed out of his mouth seemed genuine. She also came to the conclusion that Brad was doing to her what no other man had done before. He was turning her on just by looking at her.

"I don't know Brad," she said, stepping away from him. "You hurt me really bad. I've never had a man make me feel so used and abused in my life. You made me think that the entire night was just some twisted game you had constructed to get me back for telling you off. I don't know what to think. You just hurt me."

Brad got up off the couch he was now sitting on and walked towards Vanessa.

"Ness..." he said. "I know that I fucked up. I fucked up bad. This has been the worst situation I have ever put myself or even another person into, but what I'm telling you right now is the truth. I swear! Please just give me one more chance. Just give me an opportunity to make this all up to you."

Vanessa looked at the man standing in front of her who was begging for her forgiveness. She'd forgive him alright. She'd forgive him, but he was going to have to suffer first. He was going to have to go through the torment that he had put her in and she had the perfect solution for it.

"I want to believe you Brad, I truly do," she said. "But I'm standing here talking to you in a bathrobe, and this whole thing is making me feel quite uncomfortable. How about you make yourself at home for a few minutes on the couch and I'll go upstairs and tidy up a bit?"

"Uh, sure thing," Brad quickly responded, making his way back to the couch and taking a seat. "Take your time."

Vanessa quietly walked up the stairs, taking a quick look back at the sullen man sitting on her couch. She licked her lips and smiled. Brad Clark was going to get the punishment of the lifetime for what he did to her and every aching part of her body was going to thoroughly enjoy it.

Vanessa stood in front of the antique vanity admiring the reflection of herself in its mirror. She looked damn good; no one would be able to tell her otherwise. She walked towards the bed, grabbing the whip she had left there while changing. She wanted to believe the sincerity in Brad's tone of voice, but he had to give what was coming to him. Too many years had gone by in which he made Vanessa feel small and helpless. Now Brad's karma was going to come back to him threefold. Now it was time for Brad Clark to suffer.

Vanessa walked back towards the vanity, taking one last good look at herself. She never wore anything so risqué in her life for a man before, but now realized how sexy and powerful it made her feel. She originally bought the outfit to wear for Marcus that night he turned her down. She wanted to take their relationship to a new level, but obviously, his idea of a new level was getting rid of her. Memories seeped into her mind of all of the useless male encounters she had experienced in her life. Was Brad just going to be another one of them? She inhaled deeply, watching the exhales be relieved from her abdomen. She hoped not. After punishing Brad tonight, she hoped they'd be able to build a deeper connection. She was tired of playing games with men. She just wanted something real. Either way, she thought as she started towards the stairs, tonight she was going to relieve all of her sexual frustrations. Tonight she was going to be in control, and Brad was going to suffer all of the abuse she had suffered over the last few years.

She stood at the landing at the top of the stairs. She could see Brad nervously waiting for her arrival while sitting on the couch. He had no idea what he was getting himself into with her. The thought of it made Vanessa extremely horny. Here was the man who had silently put complete control over her life; who was now going to be the pawn in her game for once.

As she walked towards the last step of the staircase, she took the whip and hid it behind her back. She wanted Brad to see her dressed sexily but wanted to hide the fact that he was going to be punished for his wrongdoings. She told him that she was going to get dressed; his surprise of finding her dressed in practically nothing was enough for him to start with.

Brad looked up from his trembling hands to stare at the woman he had fallen in love standing in front of him. She had lied about getting dressed, well at least partially. Rather than put on the mundane clothing he had been considering, here she was perfectly revealing her beautiful, hourglass figure in a corset and open crotch thong. She wore long dark stockings underneath that led his eyes down to her perfectly sculpted legs that shined in the long, black stilettos that she wore. She was breathtaking, completely divine if you will.

Brad's cock that he once controlled now

stiffened hard in his jeans once more. This time around though, Brad was convinced that it would be alright to allow his body to carry on with its lustful desires. He looked into Vanessa's sultry eyes and sat in silence, a complete look of surprise gleaming over his face. In the years that he let his macho-ness take over, he had slept with many women, but none of them looked as appetizing as Vanessa did right now.

Vanessa pondered Brad's reaction, knowing that her costume was completely turning him on. She felt herself grow even wetter, just watching his eyes look into hers.

"Do you like what you see?" she asked him, still hiding the whip behind her back.

"Y...Y...Yes, absolutely," he stammered, starting to get off of the couch.

Vanessa licked her lips.

"Sit down," she demanded, now pulling the whip behind her back and cracking it across the coffee table. "You've been a very bad boy, Brad Clark. If you want my forgiveness, you are going to listen to me. Do you understand?"

Brad's eyes lit up like a child on Christmas morning. Just listening to Vanessa talk so dirty, so in control, was making beads of pre-cum form onto his dick inside of his pants. He was more than willing to become submissive to every request she had for him. The idea of her taking over was an incredible turn on and he'd do anything for her forgiveness.

"Yes Vanessa, whatever you say," he said breathlessly, taking a seat back onto the couch.

"Take off all of your clothes," she

demanded, holding the whip between both hands and cracking it yet again.

Brad undressed as if it meant facing life or death. He quickly unbuttoned his white long sleeve shirt, revealing his chiseled chest that was already soaked with sweat. Was he nervous? He pulled down his pants and threw them onto the living room floor. He sat there on the couch in silence, wearing nothing but his boxer briefs, exposing his hard penis that was twitching inside the fabric, begging to come out.

"The boxer briefs too," Vanessa demanded, cracking the whip onto the table again. "I want to see that excited cock of yours."

Without argument, Brad quickly pulled off the boxers, doing exactly what he was instructed. Vanessa smiled, admiring the compliant cock that was directed towards her. She could see the pre-cum drizzling down its shaft. She stood for a moment, just watching it.

"I want you to play with that hard dick of yours," Vanessa began, lifting her leg onto the table and revealing her swollen pussy hidden behind her panties. "I, in turn, will pleasure myself to your show."

Brad smiled and happily placed both of his hands onto his stiffened member. He used his hands to rub up in down on it, while watching Vanessa use both her hands to freely explore herself. Vanessa kept her eyes on Brad as he masturbated to her. She used her right hand to pull the corset down off her breasts, watching her tits cheerfully sit on the textile below them. Still using her right hand, she moved it down onto her left and then right breast, pulling the nipples between her fingers.

Brad was going wild on his cock, up and down. His balls bounced feverishly beneath the shaft. Vanessa wasn't quite sure if it was her power, her pleasure, or the obedient man sitting on the couch masturbating to her that was making her so hot, but she knew she had to treat the fire that was burning inside of her. She used her free hand to rub the clit of her cunt, letting out a moan that made her feel like she was going to cum.

"Come over here," she demanded, cracking the whip in Brad's direction. "Kneel before me and lick this hard clit."

Brad got off of the couch, after tugging at his cock one last time. He kept his eyes and smile on Vanessa, as he kneeled before her dripping pussy. He looked up at her while sticking his tongue, deep into her wet, warm hole. Vanessa let out a cry and shoved his head harder into her cunt with her hands. Brad licked her cunt furiously, only stopping to lick her juices that were saturating his face.

"I'm going to come," she wailed, shoving his head even deeper into her cunt. "Oh my fucking god!"

Brad held his hands around Vanessa's ass, feeling her body vibrate with each burst of her orgasm. Vanessa let go of her grip on Brad's head and smiled down at him, watching her suspect lick her juices clean off of his lips.

"Mmmm...you taste so good, Ness," he said, beaming up at her.

"Of course I do," Vanessa responded slyly.

"Now lay down. Let me fuck that stiff cock of yours."

Brad did as he was told and laid down on the plush carpet of her living room floor. Vanessa leaned over and sat down abruptly onto his cock. She bounced up and down, panting from her own heat. Brad lay stiff as he watched Vanessa work her hips further and further down onto his cock. Her breasts bounced joyously on top her chest, with each motion. She leaned over and kissed his now sensitive chest, making him scream out with desire. Brad tried to move his hands onto her hips, but Vanessa pinned them down on the floor not letting him take any control. Still leaning down, she rocked back and forth on his cock taking its entire girth into her sweet hole. Brad let out one last moan, as his cock clenched and exploded its fluids inside of her. Vanessa's cum rippled down from her like waves onto his cock. She lay on top of his body in silence, her legs trembling.

Time passed, the two still lying in silence with nothing to be heard but the music sounding from the streets. Vanessa lay on Brad's chest, using her fingers to encircle his nipples.

"Mmmm..." she said with a moan. "That was amazing."

Brad looked into her sparkling eyes and smiled.

"You're amazing, Vanessa," he said. "I'm sorry that I never admitted that to you in the first place. If I would've, things wouldn't have gotten as bad as they did between us."

Vanessa looked up at Brad and placed two

fingers onto his lips.

"Things happen for a reason," she said. "If we wouldn't have put ourselves in the situation that we did, I never would've gotten the chance to punish you."

Brad let out a laugh, grabbing Vanessa's fingers from his mouth.

"You know, Vanessa," he said. "You spent much of that time ignoring my affections. You made me suffer internally by just doing that. I think your punishment will need to come next."

Vanessa looked up and shot Brad a horny smile. She was ready for his punishment now.

4 THE WAVES OF PASSION

Susan stood in front of the mirror looking at the reflection of the morose woman who appeared before her. Her hot tears burned against her skin, ruining the makeup that she had put on that morning. How could Rodger die so young? He was only fifty-two! The pancreatic cancer came on as a surprise, one that left Rodger and Susan in great despair. Each of them had thought that Rodger's weight loss and malaise was caused by the stress he was currently facing at work. At times, Rodger complained about abdominal pain that radiated throughout his upper body, but when Susan worried, Rodger insisted that he was okay. It was only once the jaundice set in that either of them sought medical attention for Rodger's condition, but then it was too late. Rodger was at stage four pancreatic cancer, and his doctors estimated he had only two months left to live.

Susan wiped the tears from her eyes, remembering the hope that she had had originally for her husband. They had the money to afford the best medical care; it was too bad that no amount of money could afford Rodgers life. Susan, who was an advocate for natural medicine, tried every natural treatment she could find. None of them could help Rodgers condition though, both of them just had to face the fact that Rodger was dying.

After ten years of marriage, the couple had always remained hopelessly in love with each other. Susan couldn't help but feel as if she hadn't ever appreciated her husband enough. Rodger insisted that the last ten years of his life that he had spent with her were the best years of his life, but Susan was too hard on herself. She just didn't believe it; she felt like the worst wife in the world.

Rodger had always had to bend over backwards for her. None of his family, friends, or colleagues ever cared for the marriage or for Susan Hannold at all. She was too plain, too common, coming from a middle class family and attending a community college. Susan could never compare to his high class associates. She didn't go to Yale, and she didn't have a vacation home in Newport Beach; the only country club she was a part of was Rodgers, and for Christ sakes, she was only an English teacher at a suburban high school, not a doctor or lawyer like all of Rodgers acquaintances were.

Rodger had always insisted that none of those things ever mattered to him. He had a distaste for the women that came from high-class families, as all of them seemed to lack substance or intellect for that matter. He had always admired Susan's charm, her sincerity, her kind heart, and her passion to help others. The two of them would always sit together at night after a long, hard day at work and would just talk. Even after ten years, they could still look into each other's eyes and see the passion that they had shared with each other since the beginning of their relationship.

Still, Susan felt like she had never measured up. She felt as if though Rodger had just wasted the last ten years of his life on a woman who was only subpar. Marrying Susan meant Roger not associating with his family or friends very much, and when he did, he always had to hear a mouthful of bad about the woman he had chosen to marry. Living in a gated community filled with aristocrats meant Rodger didn't have the ability to leave his house without a few whispers or stares from neighbors first. Susan was like a parasite to the affluent community. They had deemed her as a woman who married a rich man for his money and nothing else.

Susan stood back from the cold, bathroom mirror and took one last look at herself. She looked like a train wreck and no ounce of make-up could save her. She twirled in the black dress she had chosen to wear for the funeral and came to the conclusion that black was going to be her new color. How could she dress in bright, beautiful clothing when Rodger's death was now going to consume her whole life? Susan took one last inhale and headed towards the direction of the door, making her way out to the solemn congregation that greeted her.

Women's voices whispered back and forth to each other as Susan made her way back into the viewing room. She sat down in the front chair, placing her eyes onto her lap rather than her husband's dead body that lie inside of a casket. There was no one there who was going to put their arm across Susan's shoulder to comfort her; no one to hug, to talk to, or to even cry to. None of Rodger's family or friends made any attempt to even speak one word to the grieving widow. Their only acknowledgement of Susan's presence was heard through whispers and felt by evil eyes.

One by one, each member of the crowd walked up to Rodgers casket and paid their respects. Susan's body sat frozen as she waited to be the last person to view her husband. She didn't want to go first. She didn't want to see him there lying dead at all. Each part of Susan's body felt numb. Susan was quite sure that her legs were going to glue themselves onto the viewing room's carpet, but somehow she managed to walk up to the casket.

Susan's eyes searched wildly at the corpse that lay before her. Minus the peppery gray wafts of hair that lined Rodger's face, his lifeless body resembled nothing of what he used to look like when he was alive. Susan could tell that they had plastered his body with make-up. His thin, frail frame was a mockery of the fit man that Susan used to know. Without warning, tears came crashing down onto Susan's face. She let out a howl that turned into shrieking, startling every guest that was standing inside of the room. She leaned over and hugged her husband's cold body, running her fingers across the now wilted skin on his face.

"Noooooo!" she screamed, hugging Rodgers corpse for dear life. "Why now? Why so soon? Why God? How could you do this to me?"

Gasps escaped from the lips of the crowd, none of them knowing quite how to react to Susan's cries. The owner of the funeral parlor and his wife rushed over to Susan's side. Timothy, Rodger's lawyer and best friend for over 20 years, was the only person to emerge from the crowd of cowards. The rest of the congregation just sat there in shock. All of them had always assumed that Susan was in the marriage for Rodgers money. All of them now assumed that she was faking it.

"Susan" Timothy pleaded, grabbing Susan away from the casket and embracing her with a hug. "Why don't we go sit in the office for a while? After everybody leaves, we'll go over the will with Rodgers family."

Susan shook her head in understanding and walked out of the room with Timothy. She could care less about her husband's will. Contrary to everyone's belief, Susan didn't marry Rodger for his money. She married him because she loved him with all of her heart and soul. Now her heart was shattered, and her soul was taken by Rodger on the night he took his last breath.

Susan lay on the silk sheets of her bed

wearing the black chemise that Rodger had bought for her on their anniversary. She rubbed her hands over her breasts, remember Rodger's last touch. Susan may have been two hundred and fifty million dollars rich, but she'd give it all away if it meant sharing one last passionate night with her now deceased husband.

It had been two months since Rodger died, each day since providing no relief to Susan. Having such strong work ethic, Susan never used any of her vacation days offered by the school district. Twelve years of working there without time off proved to be useful in one way. Scott Baird, the superintendent, proved to have a heart after all, offering Susan the last three months of the school year off. Susan originally considered that with three paid months off and three months off for summer vacation, she would have all of the time in the world to get over her grief for her loss, but the time off proved otherwise.

Susan found herself an awkward mess, spending most of her time crying and unable to get out of bed. Everything in the house reminded her of Rodger. It didn't help that their shared closet still smelled of his cologne. Rodger's belongings still sat neatly placed inside of the house. Susan was hell-bent on keeping everything down to his body wash that still sat inside of their shower. Susan found herself wearing his nightshirts each time she went to bed, even finding herself smoking his cigars just to smell their scent. Everything in the house reminded Susan of the love that they once shared, now lost.

Everything seemed to be asking Susan why she still chose to still live.

Enough is enough, Susan thought to herself. Why do I stay here? Rodger would not want to see me live my life so miserably. Before he died, he even told me so, so why I am doing this to myself? Nobody likes me here. I have no family or friends. The only thing I have is my career, but can't I be an English schoolteacher in any part of the country? Why here? Why where I am most miserable?

Susan got up off the bed and threw on her velour robe. She walked down the stairs into Rodgers office and sat down at the desk, turning on his computer. She didn't want to spend the rest of her life being hopeless and downtrodden. She was only a forty-year-old woman; her life didn't have to be over. If Susan was going to make a new life for herself, she could find all of the tools to start by using the internet. Susan looked at the picture frame that sat on Rodger's desk. She smiled and blew a kiss at the happy couple that it showcased. I love you Rodger, but it's time to move on. I promise that you will always be in my heart.

Susan took a big whiff of the warm, California air. The ocean breeze was salty; nothing like the cool, crisp air of New Hampshire that Susan was used to, but something about it was refreshing. Susan sat down on the balcony and took a large gulp from her glass of wine. Everything about this move was refreshing. Although new and scary in some ways, Susan decided that the move was the best thing she could've ever done for herself. Rodger would've wanted her happiness, and right now, that's all that Susan was hoping to rediscover. Staying in New Hampshire would've meant subjecting herself to the same snooty aristocrats that would've continued to turn her unhappiness into misery.

Even Susan deciding to move seemed to stir up the circle. In the small town, word traveled fast, and the day that movers showed up at Susan's residence loading boxes was the day that the town turned into an uproar. Susan could not leave the house without feeling the harsh eyes glaring at her behind her back. When she went to go do errands, she'd hear the women whispering behind her. Everybody thought that she was in it for the money, and now with Rodger dead, it would be typical of her to pick up and leave with everything. It didn't help that Susan was the only person in Rodgers will. That left his family and friends feeling cheated and mostly suspicious of Susan, as if she changed Rodgers will herself.

Susan took another sip of her wine and sighed. Nobody here knew her yet. She could finally live in a town without rumors, roaming eyes, and nosy neighbors. She could go outside, get her mail, and not feel like she was being watched the entire time while doing it. She could go to the grocery store, only to find smiles instead of frowns. Rodger dying was the worst thing that had ever happened to Susan, but moving to California was going to be one of the best decisions that Susan had made for herself in a long time.

There was a knock at the door. Susan sat still, a puzzled expression on her face. Who on Earth was at the front door? Susan had only been here for a day now. She hadn't met anybody yet, not even a neighbor. Nobody that Susan knew previously had any idea where she lived, let alone what state she moved to. Susan finished the last of the wine left in the glass and walked into the house. She hesitantly walked down the stairs headed towards the front door. A tall, slender woman with long, curly brown hair greeted her.

"Hi," the woman said joyously. "I'm Ellen, your next-door neighbor. I saw that you moved in last night and wanted to welcome you to the neighborhood. It was too late then, so I thought I'd stop by this afternoon. I hope you're a sweets girl as much as I am. I brought you some fresh-baked brownies."

Susan nervously grabbed the box from the woman's hands. The woman had caught her off guard in just her bathrobe, but she seemed friendly enough. Hell, she was friendlier than any of Susan's neighbors in New Hampshire. None of them welcomed her to the neighborhood when she first moved in. Most of them gawked at her in disgust. The rumors started the day she walked into her husband's front door.

"Hi Ellen" Susan replied. "It's very nice to meet you. I'm Susan Hannold. I just moved here from New Hampshire so it's very exciting to finally meet someone from the neighborhood. I don't know anybody here yet."

Susan stood back from the door motioning for the woman to come in. She anxiously chewed at her lip, feeling slightly embarrassed that she made herself sound so desperate for a friend.

"Do you have a husband?" Ellen asked while taking a seat on Susan's sectional.

"I did" Susan said grimly, taking a seat next her. "He died recently. That's part of the reason why I decided to move to La Jolla."

"Oh you poor thing!" Ellen exclaimed, placing an arm around Susan's shoulder. "I'm sorry about your loss. I hope my asking didn't offend you."

"No, not at all" Susan assured her. "For the first time since his death, I finally feel okay about it. Of course, I still grieve for him, but it's time to move on, you know?"

Ellen sat back into the chair and smiled a warm smile at Susan.

"So why La Jolla?" she asked with wondering eyes.

"Well..."Susan began, smiling back at her. "I've always dreamed of going to California. The Californian dream I guess. When Rodger died, New Hampshire offered nothing for me anymore. We... well I didn't have many friends there. I never really fit in, I guess. I was too middle class, too average, I guess. La Jolla just seemed like a nice change of pace for me after doing some research. Close to the beach, yet small. I wanted something kind of comfortable and it was easy enough to find a new job here online."

"Yeah, La Jolla is a great place to live" said Ellen passionately. "It's very comfortable. I think it will be a great place for someone like you to start out again. You'll make friends easily here. Everybody, for the most part, is friendly."

"That's exactly what I need" Susan concurred.

"Well, hey, I know a great way to start!" Ellen said excitedly. "My husband and I are throwing a BBQ tomorrow. We'll have a lot of our friends there, lots of people from the neighborhood. It would be a great way for you to get to meet everybody. Why don't you come?"

"I'll be there" Susan said, finally feeling like she was able to breathe again.

It was 11:30 am and Susan woke up feeling restless. She spent much of the night worrying about whether or not the people at Ellen's party would like her. She wanted to make a great first impression. She'd be meeting fellow neighbors after all, and the last thing Susan wanted was to live in a neighborhood filled with whispers and talk again. She spent most of the time last night trying to figure out what exactly she was going to wear. Being from New Hampshire, LL Bean seemed to be the standby for women's attire, but from seeing the locals, Susan knew that breezy, comfortable pieces were in. After rummaging through old boxes of summer clothes that were packed long before the move or Rodger's death even, Susan finally found what she was going to wear. There sitting crumpled in the bottom of the box was a white cotton summer dress with blue, paisley details. Susan knew that this would be the dress to make that first great impression of her, and after putting it on, she knew how killer it made her body look.

Susan got up out of bed and put the summer dress that she had picked out the night before on. She felt fantastic and excited to start her day, even with the little sleep that she got from last night. She did a twirl in front of the mirror, smiling at the long, smooth legs that shined back at her. Normally, Susan would find herself in a bathrobe sipping a mug of coffee in the morning, but today Susan felt different, she felt changed. Susan headed towards her master bathroom and sat down at her vanity. Since Rodger's funeral, Susan stopped applying make-up to her face. She only really ever did it to make herself look more beautiful. Without Rodger alive, Susan found no point in impressing anyone.

Having been invited to a BBQ with people attending that Susan never met before was a good enough excuse to make herself look and feel more alive. She dusted her brushes inside of the mineral powder and went to work. The final result, Susan had to admit, was breath taking. She looked absolutely radiant.

Susan spent the rest of the early afternoon baking. Ellen never said she had to bring a dish to the party, but Susan was persistent on making a damn good impression. One thing Susan knew besides the English language was cooking. She was a self-proclaimed top chef and knew once putting her cherry almond tart into the oven that it was going to be to die for. Nobody at the party was going to dislike her for her culinary skills. Susan grabbed her keys, tart in hand, and made it out the door.

When moving into her new house, Susan fell in love with Ellen's before she met her. She almost felt cheated by the price that she had paid for her new home in La Jolla when she saw her new neighbors. Although Susan was looking for something quainter, much less extravagant than the home she had shared with Rodger, three quarters of a million dollars seemed ridiculous in comparison to Ellen's.

The home was enormous. It was quite obvious that there were at least 8 different bedrooms in it. While walking towards the back of the home to reach the yard, Susan admired the beautiful landscaping that surrounded it. Succulents and plants from origins that seemed unknown to Susan, lined the walkway. Susan reached the marble patio in the back, her focal point on the built in fireplace. Of course, the crowds of smiling faces greeting Susan we're nice to look at as well. Susan's mouth dropped when she saw a banner hanging on the back of the house. It read: Welcome to the neighborhood, Susan!

"Susan!" Ellen exclaimed, rushing through the crowd towards her. "I'm glad you made it. I would've felt silly with this banner hanging here if you didn't show."

"You didn't have to do this all for me, Ellen" Susan said bashfully, while embracing Ellen with a hug.

"Of course I did!" Ellen exclaimed. "After all that you've gone through with your husband passing, you deserve a warm welcome to your new life."

Susan clung on to Ellen, wondering if she'd ever let go. Tears formed in her eyes as she thought how surreal this all was. The last ten years of Susan's life had been spent on trying to compete and never measuring up. In the last three days of her new life, Susan felt more welcomed than she had ever felt in New Hampshire. Susan unlocked from the hug and wiped her eyes, hiding the fact that she was crying tears of joy.

"I brought my world-famous cherry almond tart" she said, showing the dish to Ellen.

"Oh you shouldn't have Susan!" Ellen proclaimed, placing her arm around Susan and walking her towards the crowd. "This looks so delish! Let's put this on the table, and I'll introduce you to everybody."

Butterflies rumbled in Susan Hannold's stomach as she shook hands, hugged, and greeted each individual at the party. Everyone was interested in finding out more about Susan's life prior to living in La Jolla. Nobody had asked if she was married, making Susan suspect that Ellen had told everybody about her husband's death before her arrival. All of the women of the party took it upon themselves to compliment Susan on her dress. They took it upon themselves to compliment Susan on practically everything about herself, making her feel good, a feeling Susan realized she hadn't felt in a very long time.

Lots of the men at the party were flirtatious

with Susan, making her giddy like a young schoolgirl again. There was only one man in the crowd that Susan simply did not like, Travis. He was loud and obnoxious, his bad qualities increasing with each drink that he had made at the bar. For the life of her, Susan couldn't understand why Ellen would even associate with a man of his character. His childish nature was quickly recognized as an annoyance by Susan almost immediately. After learning that Travis was an old friend of Ellen's and not of her husband Ethan's, everything about his presence became clear. Ellen obviously kept him around because of his good looks.

For being thirty-nine, Travis resembled that of a man who was thirty. He was extremely ripped. His shape, he claimed, came from surfing. His face was as clear and soft as porcelain. Susan wondered if the Californian sun, boasting its large amounts of Vitamin D, was to blame. Perhaps staying in shape and eating fresh seafood helped in graceful aging as well. Besides his fitness or complexion, Susan didn't find the rest of his looks to be that attractive. Yet, somehow, his teenage-styled hair spiked up with gel seemed slightly irresistible to her.

Susan decided that there were enough people at the party to immense herself with. She could easily avoid Travis like the plague. At least, she thought so, until Ellen and her husband invited her over to play horseshoes. Being a respectable guest meant joining in on the fun. Susan didn't know how to play horseshoes, but she was more than willing to learn. How could she say no to Ellen or to the rest of the guests when they threw such a lovely party in her honor?

Ellen told Susan that the game would be easy to learn and played a sample game against Ethan first. When Susan's turn was up, she wasn't sure if it was luck or just the draw of the odds, but Ellen decided to pin her up against Travis. Susan quickly caught on and the crowd quickly grew dull. Everyone moved back over to the bar to make a round of new drinks, leaving Susan and Travis playing a game of their own.

"I know that you don't like me Susan" said Travis out of nowhere, taking a glance at the last person to leave from spectating their game. "I really can't put my finger on why, but it's obvious that you've been avoiding me tonight. Am I correct?"

Susan took a large gulp from her glass and pitched a horseshoe at the stake.

"Hmm..." She began, coyly. "You're good at catching on. It's not necessarily that I don't like you Travis. I guess I'm just not used to someone like your kind. I'm from New Hampshire after all."

"Yea, well that's not really an excuse to be a bitch towards me" Travis huffed. "I like you, Susan. At least you should give me a chance."

Susan threw another horseshoe, losing herself in her own thoughts. What exactly did Travis mean in saying that he liked her? Did he just like her...or did he like her, like her? Susan felt the familiar sensation of butterflies again. Half of the party, Susan spent time finding a million and one reasons why she didn't like Travis. Why did all of a sudden she feel this way towards him?

"How about this?" Travis proposed, interrupting the silence between them. "If I lose the game, I'll never bother you again. I'll make sure to never show up at the same functions that you will, and if I do, I'll keep my interaction with you limited. But if I win, you have to give me a chance. I know that you're new to California and probably never surfed a day in your life, but I'm a surf coach and if I win you have to get a free lesson from me."

Susan stood for a moment, thinking again. It was clear that Travis "liked her, liked her."

"You're on," she said quickly.

Just then, Travis threw his last horseshoe, clearly winning the game.

Susan wasn't quite sure if it was the bottomless glass of whiskey or the fact that she had experienced so much adoration from male admirers that night of the party, but when she came home, she was feeling frisky. She walked into her bedroom and looked one last time at her silhouette in the white dress, feeling horny for the stiffened nipples that reflected back at her.

Near the end of Rodgers life, his cancer made him so weak that he couldn't make passionate love to her anymore. At that time, sex was one of the last things Susan was thinking about, but now that time passed, Susan realized that it had been a long time since she had been touched by a man. It had been a long time since she had been pleasured, period.

Susan drunkenly searched through the

unpacked boxes in her bedroom. She clearly remembered packing her lingerie and sex toys into one of the boxes. A smile beamed across her face as she pulled out her large dildo from one of the boxes. She was going to need this tonight.

Susan tore off her sundress, standing there in nothing but her laced, white panties. She placed her hands over her large breasts, gently massaging small circles around them until she reached her nipples. She looked at the puffy little nipples and pulled at them playfully with each hand. Her mind flashed pictures of Travis massaging them instead, first with his hands and later with his mouth. Susan felt her panties become increasingly wet. A fire burned within her body, yearning to rub her clit. She sat on the edge of her bed and rubbed wildly between the slits, imagining Travis' mouth doing all of the work for her. Fluids gushed all over her fingers, Susan envisioning Travis licking it up with his tongue.

As Susan's visions grew increasingly vivid, she felt herself yearning to feel Travis' dick inside of her. She used the thick dildo to freely rub up and down on her clit, imagining Travis teasing her excitedly. Susan let out a cry, almost feeling herself cum instantly and pushed the dildo deep inside of her pussy instead. She used one hand to ravish her nipples, while the other hand forcefully slammed the pretend cock inside of her. The pressure of her hand rubbed forcefully against her clit, making her pussy cream on the silicone dildo. Susan let out a howl, now jumping up and down on the cock. She let out one last scream, calling out Travis' name in passion.

Susan sat still for a while on the edge of the bed, the faux cock still deep inside of her dripping cunt. She was mortified. Fucking herself felt like cheating on Rodger, mostly because she fucked herself thinking of another man.

Two weeks went by before Susan decided to pick up the phone and take Travis up on his offer for surfing lessons. Ellen had been bugging her for days to give him a chance now, and although Susan still felt regret for pleasuring herself with him in mind, she gave in to her friend's pleads. Perhaps it was too soon for her to move on and find another man, but there would be no harm done in getting a free surfing lesson. Ellen had told her that she and Travis had been friends for twenty years now. Obviously, a friendship could form between them; it didn't have to be sexual. That is if Susan could have the strength to not give in to her lust for him.

Susan picked up the phone, feeling her hands shaking as she dialed each number. As the phone began to ring, Susan felt the strong urge to hang it up before Travis answered. Maybe, this was a big mistake? Susan could feel heat rising in her waist as she envisioned what Travis' dick would like glistening with his sweat.

"Hey, Travis speaking" the man on the other line answered. "How can I help you?"

"Travis?" Susan questioned, feeling silly even asking because she knew exactly who she was calling. "Hey it's Susan. We met at Ellen's party. I was calling about the free..."

"Surfing lesson?" Travis interrupted with a laugh. "Hi, Susan. How are you? I was wondering when you were going to take me up on my offer."

"Yeah, I've been busy" Susan lied. "But I've been doing some thinking and realized that it's been a while since I got some fitness in. I think surfing might be right up my alley. When would be a good day to schedule the lesson?"

"How about now?" Travis asked, leaving Susan startled on the other line.

"Now?" Susan asked, playing with the cord of the phone nervously. "Um...yeah...sure. Can you give me like fifteen minutes?"

"Take all the time you need doll face" Travis replied. "I'll be here."

Susan rushed up the stairs once hanging up the phone, and stumbled her way to her closet. She had to find something to wear now, and she had to find it fast! She pulled out her black bikini and threw it on without even taking a glance at herself in the mirror. She wanted to look tied together, but not like she tried hard to do it. Even though the pit in her stomach was telling her that she was swooning over the fact that she was meeting with the man of her wet dreams, Susan tried to deny it. She threw on a pair of skinny black jeans and a tank to match her casual look, throwing her hair into a messy ponytail after. She flew back down the stairs and headed straight out the door. Travis may have told her to take her time, but Susan was hell bent on having her surfing lesson now.

Travis' house was not at all what Susan had expected. She imagined him living in some run down shack on the beach, not a beautiful mansion for a beach house. Palm trees and tropical plants lined that terrace, which also featured a perfectly placed gazebo. The house was built on a slope directly off of the beach and displayed two balconies, one off of each floor, facing the water. Susan walked up the stone path that led to the front door and stopped. She took a deep inhale of the ocean air into her lungs, lifting her hand to knock at a door that was already opening. Travis looked at the tense woman standing on his doorstep and greeted her with a smile.

"Hi Susan" he said, motioning for Susan to come into his house. "Thanks for coming. You look lovely today."

"Thanks" Susan responded, eyeing up the nautical décor in his living room. "Some place you have here Travis. It's really nice."

"Thanks" Travis replied, leading Susan to his built in bar. "Care for a drink? It might take the edge off with you being a beginner and all."

"Sure" Susan responded, pretending not to eye up Travis' package that now was stiffened in his blue denim jeans. "Whiskey on the rocks."

Travis happily poured the drinks for his guest and himself, humming a sandy tune as he poured. Susan nervously made conversation, trying to keep her eyes on her glass rather than Travis' hardened cock that was beckoning her. She was sure that Travis had caught her a few times throughout their conversation eyeing him up. She was sure his excited member was happily skyrocketing because of her presence. Why else would he be so hard just talking to a woman that he only was going to give surfing lessons to?

Travis led Susan to his back door that followed out onto the beach. Susan stood in silence just taking in the beauty of the waves rushing against the smooth, white sand. She finished up her glass of whiskey while Travis went into his shed to pull out the surfboards they were going to use for his lesson. When he came back, he was surprised to see Susan still standing there on the beach wearing her clothes.

"Don't tell me you're one of those women who plans on surfing with jeans and a tank on" he laughed. "I promise I won't focus on your body. Your lesson won't go as smoothly with you wearing all of that bulk in the water."

"Oh I'm not" Susan replied, trying to hide the burn in her cheeks from embarrassment. "I just got lost in the horizon. That's all."

Susan pulled the tank top over her head, exposing her luscious breasts that hung perfectly inside of the triangle bikini top. The top offered all of the support a woman could ask for, but at the same time exposed enough cleavage to drive any man wild. Susan could feel Travis' eyes behind her, scanning her body as she pulled off her jeans. Although still feeling slightly guilty, Susan secretly jiggled her butt for Travis to see. There was no harm in a little flirtation.

"You know Susan..." Travis began as he walked towards her. "For someone who says they haven't worked out in a while, you're pretty fit."

"I stay in shape" Susan responded slickly, grabbing a board from Travis' hand. "Let's do this thing."

Travis defiantly knew his way around on a board. Sarah learned that he had been surfing ever since he could walk. Both of his parents were avid surfers, and his mother used to place him on the board as she rode the waves. Susan also learned that her first impressions of Travis were incorrect, besides the fact that she found him attractive, which she was now realizing how increasingly he was becoming during their lesson. Travis was sweet and caring, not to mention funny and smart. Teaching surfing lessons was something that he did in his free time. His real career was being a biochemist and the man knew his way around all of the terminology, impressing Susan even more.

The only thing that Susan learned during their lesson was how to stand on the board. Travis tried to convince Susan that she was quick leaner and that to further advance as a surfer it would take time, but Susan tried to dismiss his charm, thinking that she did a horrible job. Susan walked to the pile of her crumpled clothes that sat on the beach and started to put her black jeans back on after toweling off. Travis stood beside her putting on his dark denim jeans. He focused on Susan's body, admiring how great she looked. The distraction not only made him rock hard, but made his body loose balance while pulling up his pants. Travis fell over backwards into the sand.

"Are you okay?" Susan asked while rushing over to Travis' side.

She lay on top of his body opening the lids of his closed eyes. Travis started laughing, embracing her waist with his strong, sculpted arms.

"I'm such an idiot sometimes," he said. "I was focusing more on you getting dressed than myself."

"You perv!" Susan teased, secretly flattered that Travis had focused his attention on her. "You told me that if I lose you'd give me a free swimming lesson, not that you'd attempt to seduce me."

Travis looked deeply into Susan's glistening eyes.

"I didn't attempt to seduce you yet" Travis said slyly. "But I will now, if you don't mind."

Susan had no time to speak. She couldn't think, let alone take action to stop Travis from planting his lips onto hers. He pressed his lips gently against Susan's, searching for her agreement with his tongue. Susan licked Travis' lips, sending shivers down her spine. He tasted of the salt from the waters of the ocean. She could taste the faint leftovers of his gin and tonic as well. Something about the two flavors sent heat waves throughout Susan's body. The taste was of a masculine descent. The taste was fun.

Travis used his hands to roll over Susan's body, her back now pinned down against the sand. He moved his mouth away from Susan's, now licking up and down her neck. Susan moaned, feeling the tingling sensation send chills throughout her body due to Travis teasing her erogenous zone. Travis hummed, moving his mouth and tongue further down Susan's body. He cupped both of her breasts with his hands and removed them from the fabric of her bikini top, exposing her perky tits to the air. Travis's tongue rolled across each nipple, and then flicked gently across the sensitive skin. Susan's chest rose in response to the sensation. Susan's eyes roamed down to the man who was performing on her breasts below. She could feel the surge of hormones race throughout her body. Watching Travis tantalize her breasts was creating saturation inside her pants.

"You're making me so wet" Susan blurted out while looking at him.

Travis looked up from Susan's large tits and smiled, licking his lips. He gave her a look as if though he was saluting her and traveled his tongue to her stomach, where he ran circles around it. He moved his hands down to Susan's pants and pulled them down off of her feet. Susan looked down at the man, not knowing for sure what he was going to do next. She moved her hands down to her moist pussy that hid inside of the bikini bottoms and began rubbing her clit outside of the fabric. Travis smiled and grabbed at his dick, groaning with excitement while watching her masturbate. He reached over and pulled down

Susan's bottoms, exposing the neatly trimmed cunt that was awaiting his arrival. He leaned over and kissed the top of the mound playfully, inhaling its sweet, fresh scent. Using a free hand, he spread the lips of the cunt and inserted his tongue inside of it. He licked at Susan's clit hungrily, sucking up all of the hot juices of her cunt inside of his mouth. His tongue slid down to Susan's dripping hole where he forcefully pushed his tongue inside and out. Susan spread her legs wider, playing with her clit while Travis inserted his tongue.

Susan wailed in ecstasy, thinking of how amazing it felt to have Rodger perform oral on her again. A sick feeling sat inside of Susan's stomach. This wasn't Rodger. Rodger was dead. What the hell was she doing? Susan sat up quickly, pushing Travis off of her lap.

"I have to go" She said, reaching for her clothes wildly.

Travis sat on his knees, baffled by Susan's reaction. He thought that she had liked him. Every woman that he ever slept with told him that he was a master at performing oral on them. Did he do something wrong?

"Wait...Susan!" Travis pleaded with the frazzled woman who was getting dressed. "Did something happen? Did we move too fast? I have no problem stopping and taking it slow. You don't have to leave."

"Travis" Susan started, guilt engulfing her body. "I can't do this. This whole thing is a mistake. I'm sor...."

Susan turned her head to wipe the tears that were streaming from her eyes. She couldn't let Travis see her cry. She couldn't give him one last look either. The whole thing was a mistake. Not only was she embarrassed and felt guilt for wasting Travis' time, she felt guilt for cheating on her husband and enjoying it. She ran from the beach, not stopping until she reached her car, leaving Travis still sitting on the beach bewildered.

Susan lay in bed, a victim. She was a victim to her own emotions and a victim to her own self. The feeling was starting to get old for Susan who was now realizing after locking herself in two days of personal reflection that she had spent the last decade of her life not feeling worthy. She never felt like she could ever match up to any of the other women in New Hampshire. Rodger's circle of friends was all wealthy, most of them coming from old money. Their wives sat on a pedestal, taken care of by their husbands or their fathers' wealth. None of them expected plain Susan to come along. None of them wanted to accept a woman who didn't want to wear high-end clothing or go to weekly salon visits; none of them wanted to accept a career woman, especially one who worked when she didn't need to.

Susan didn't feel pretty enough around those women; she never believed when her husband called her beautiful. She always felt so empty, and she always talked to herself in a negative fashion.

Susan moved to California because she

thought by getting away from the people who looked down upon her that she'd be able to find her self-confidence again, but she was wrong. It wasn't an issue of beauty this time or an issue regarding her career choice. Susan felt content in both of those aspects about herself since coming to California, but now she lacked the confidence to move on. Each time Susan told herself that she was ready to move on from Rodgers death was a moment in which Susan was lying.

When Rodger and Susan both knew that Rodger was dying, Susan never pondered the idea of meeting another man, but Rodger did. Susan's thoughts flooded to Rodger's last dying days in which he pulled Susan down on his chest towards him and told her just how much that he loved her. He also, Susan recalled, told her that she was still very much a young, beautiful woman. He didn't want her to waste the rest of her life mourning for him. He didn't want her to waste the rest of her life lonely. Susan assured him that she would never be able to love again, that no man would be able to replace the shoes that Rodger wore, but Rodger intervened. He loved his wife and that meant he wanted her to be happy. Although he had originally thought that when saying their wedding vows - including death do us part - that their death would've came at a later age, he knew he was leaving a wife that could be guaranteed at least another thirty years of her life.

Susan pleaded and most importantly, Susan continued mourning, forgetting Rodger's last thoughts. Instead, she continued down the path she always took herself, a path that led to negative self-talk and irrational thinking. She felt as if she didn't deserve to ever be happy again, as if being happy without Rodger was a curse. She didn't want to cheat on the man that she once loved and although Rodger was dead now it still felt like cheating.

Her body laid hollow inside, but there was still a spark of flame that resided within it. Travis was a great man, a caring man, a compassionate man, an interesting man to say at the least. Rodger had always been good looking, but Travis' looks were impressive in comparison. While Rodger's passing still tore at Susan's heartstrings, Travis' stiffened tongue running down her body left her feeling conflicted. Rodger told her that he wanted her to feel comfortable with seeing another man, that he wanted her to find happiness, but Susan was torn. She buried her hands into her face and screamed, barely hearing the doorbell go off.

Susan jumped out of bed. Could it be Ellen? Susan was sure by now that Travis might have told her what had happened between them. She probably was coming over to check on Susan and see if she was okay. Ellen was turning into the best friend that Susan never had before, but she didn't feel comfortable with pouring her heart and soul out to her yet. She would just have to make up some lame excuse, like being sick, for not wanting to invite Ellen in. If she just ignored the doorbell, Ellen might worry being that her car was parked outside.

"Coming," Susan hollered, making her way

down the steps.

A feeling of lightheadedness overcame her when she opened the door to Travis standing on her front porch instead of Ellen.

"Can we talk?" Travis asked nervously while scanning the fragile woman at the door.

Susan was speechless, leaving a moment of silence in between them.

"Sure" she replied, shakiness in her voice. "Come in."

Travis stood sullen while watching Susan take a seat onto the couch.

"What happened back there?" he asked, cutting to the chase. "I thought you had felt the passion that I did. I mean, it seemed like you gave into it anyways. I'm sorry if I went too far, but you could've asked me to stop instead of running away from me. I would've understood if you wanted to take things slow. You kind of just left me like a fool standing there on the beach like that."

Susan sat in disbelief, raising her hands to her head and cupping it with her fingers. She felt terrible inside for leaving Travis the way she did, but she never expected him to confront her like that. She felt Travis' eyes linger at her from across the room and lifted her head from her hands. A buzzing sound came from the kitchen, reminding Susan of the teakettle that she had forgotten.

"Tea?" Susan asked, standing up from the couch.

Travis responded to Susan's question with a murky expression upon his face.

"I'm not much of a tea drinker," he admitted. "But I do like coffee, if making it would be much trouble for you."

"Not at all," Susan responded, reaching the doorframe of the kitchen and pointing towards the doors of her patio. "Why don't you take a seat outside? I'll bring some fresh coffee right out for you and we can continue to talk about this."

"Sure," Travis replied hesitantly, making his way out of the door.

Travis sunk down into the wicker patio chair and inhaled a breath of the fresh ocean air. Susan had a beautiful home with a nice view. It might not have been on the beach, but it was a beautiful Californian home. He turned the seat around when he caught a glimpse of Ethan, Ellen's husband. He had not told him or Ellen about the situation that had occurred between him and Susan, and he wanted to keep it that way. If Ethan caught him sitting on Susan's patio, he would be bound to invite himself over, not realizing the matter that needed to be resolved between Travis and Susan.

"Here's your coffee" Susan announced as she slid the glass doors closed, entering the patio. "I hope you like sugar and cream."

"Yea that's exactly how I like it" Travis replied, leaving Susan questioning the sultriness in his tone of voice. "Hey would you mind if we went back inside? Ethan is out in the yard, and I'd really rather him not notice us. I'd really like to talk alone together."

"Well I want to be outside" Susan beamed while licking her lower lip as she examined the muscles ripping out of Travis' shirt. "But I have a balcony off of the master bedroom. We could go upstairs and sit out there. It looks the opposite direction of Ellen and Ethan's house."

"Sounds like a plan" Travis said excitedly, grabbing his coffee cup off of the table. "Lead the way."

By the end of the conversation, Susan was finding it extremely hard to ignore the sexual tension that was building up inside of her. Travis' dimples that formed in his cheeks while he smiled his gracious smile were enough to make her heart melt. His biceps continued to tease her each time that he moved his arms, begging to be torn at by Susan's lustful hands. Each time that Travis took a sip from his coffee, Susan watched his lips gently press against the mug, his tongue secretly licking up the drips that fell from the cup. Susan felt her panties begin to moisten. Oh, how she wished those lips would passionately embrace her. Oh how she desired to feel his warm, attentive tongue flick against her swollen clit.

What really mattered most though was that he listened. He kept his eyes on Susan intently throughout the conversation. He felt sorrow, empathy, and compassion for her as she unfolded the terrible nightmare that had stricken her with her recent husband's death. He understood her hesitation for wanting to move forward so soon with another man. He promised to wait for her. Best of all, he had no hurry. Susan felt like a special package wrapped up hiding a surprise. Travis would wait for her no matter how long it took. She wasn't just a piece of ass to him. He desired her body, as much as he desired her affection. His admiration was different from most men. He truly liked her.

Susan felt her stomach jitter as she moved closer into the table. She found herself gazing into Travis' deep, dark, sparkling eyes. It may be the cry of an animal instinct, but Susan could no longer withhold her yearning for this man. She placed her cup of tea onto the table and positioned herself on top of the flat surface, embracing Travis' mouth with her lips. Travis moaned as he felt the object of his desires take full control of his body. She lavishly sucked on his lips, teasing them with her tongue in between. Travis pulled her in closer to him, feeling her large bust press against his. He moaned, feeling himself stiffen in his pants.

Silky, soft arms pulled Travis up from his chair. Susan ripped off his shirt, popping buttons off in the heat of the moment. She positioned herself to sit up on the glass patio table, wrapping her legs tightly around Travis' waist. His abs and chest muscles glistened in the sun, driving Susan wild as she violently licked them. She teased each nipple with her tongue, smiling each time Travis leaned back and let out a heavy moan. Her hips grinded further into Travis', causing her to let out cries of passion as she felt his hard member thrust against her. She wanted his hard cock badly.

"Let's go inside," Susan whispered into Travis' ear. "I have something I'm dying to give you."

Travis chucked and scooped the woman up with his arms. He carried her like a barbarian, rushing through the glass doors of the balcony and placing her body with force onto the bed. He stood before her and stared at her wildly.

"You are so sexy," Susan laughed. "Now, I suggest that you pull down those pants of yours."

Travis did as he was instructed and pulled down his pants. He questioned whether or not he should leave his boxer briefs on, but Susan made that decision for him as she wildly used her hands to pull them down herself. All that stood between them now was his rock hard cock. Travis was unsure how to use it at the moment, but again found his question answered for him as he watched Susan take the whole member into her mouth. She bobbed up and down on it, teasing his balls with her hands. Travis let out a growl, his eyes rolling back in his head, as he experienced the ecstasy of Susan's mouth. It was so wet and tightly wrapped around his cock. This, by far, was the hottest blowjob that Travis had ever been given.

Susan sucked for some time, continuing to tease his balls with her hand while using the free hand of hers to play with her clit. The wet juices of Susan's pussy streamed down her fingers; blowing Travis was not only exhilarating but it was making her feel dirty. Feeling dirty for Susan meant instantly wanting to cum. She crammed two of her fingers deep inside of her pussy, pushing them in and out, as she hoped Travis' cock soon would. She lifted her hips and began riding her fingers, sucking on Travis' dick even wilder. Travis took his hands and used them to move Susan's mouth off of his cock. If she kept doing that he was going to cum. Travis decided he'd much rather cum in her hot cunt. The smell of her pussy was so enticing that it was making Travis feel rabid.

"I need you to stop," Travis said politely. "I want to make love to you, and if you keep that up, I won't get the chance."

Susan looked up at Travis and smiled at him. She wiped the saliva that had built from giving the blowjob off of her face and lay down on the sheets of her bed spread eagle. Travis jumped on the bed and laid on top of Susan, spreading her pussy lips to make room for his cock. He stretched her legs out even further, feeling the stretch of Susan's muscles further embracing his cock. She was wet and best of all she was tight. It was clear that she hadn't been sexually active for some time now. Travis thrust in and out of Susan watching her breasts tease him with their jiggle with each motion of his dick. He savagely pulled at Susan's top uncovering the unsheathed breasts that lay underneath it. Puffy pink nipples greeted him; Travis decided to greet them with his tongue.

The nipples hardened from the sensation of wetness and toying. Susan felt her pussy fill up with juices as Travis happily sucked her nipples. She let out a sound of the wild as she creamed all over Travis's cock. Travis, still sucking her nipples, came inside of Susan's hot cunt. He continued to plunge deep inside of Susan's pussy, letting out each remaining droplet of his cum. Susan let out one last groan and embraced the collapsed man with a

kiss.

"Thank you," she whispered into his ear.

"No, thank you," Travis responded. "That was amazing."

The terror of Susan's dreams left her in confusion and pleasure. She felt her pussy gush juices down her legs as Rodger pushed one final deep plunge inside of her. Susan awoke, her eyes wide open, recalling the entirety of her dream. Sweat poured down her body. She had never had a dream in her life that wasn't a dream but an actual memory.

She remembered how Rodger unbuttoned her blouse and passionately pulled down her skirt, undressing her for the bath that he had filled for her in celebration of their anniversary. The water was lined with rose petals, the air filled with a sweet lavender scent. Even after nine years of being married together, Rodger still treated her as well as he did when they first met. He pulled off her panties and unhooked her bra, planting little kisses across her skin while doing so. Rodger took Susan's hand and led her to the tub; where she sunk into the bubbles and rose petals he had spent weeks planning for her. Susan relaxed in the warm water, feeling the tingling sensation calming down her sore muscles. Rodger sat on the edge of the tub and poured warmed massage oil over her breasts. The heat of the oil sent shockwaves down Susan's spine. She smiled up from closed eyes and looked hungrily at her husband as he worked the oil onto her breasts. His firm hands felt good across the sensitive skin, making Susan's nipples push out in excitement. Rodger leaned down and sucked them tenderly, pushing his hands across her stomach and onto her enlarged clit.

His fingers gently teased Susan's pussy, her aching body wanting to feel every inch of him. Rodger smiled at his pleased wife and released his fingers from her. He gathered a loofah and moisturizing body wash in his hands, proceeding to wash his wife's heat stricken body head to toe. Rodger had always made Susan feel like a princess, but his teasing ways began to make her feel wicked. As much as she appreciated her husband washing her, she wanted to feel his hands on her inside their bed sheets. She wanted most to feel her husband inside of her.

Rodger could see the anxiousness displayed on his wives face. He smiled at himself knowing how much he pleased her and grabbed a towel to dry her off. Susan could barely make it to the bedroom standing on her own two feet. Her legs were trembling as they recalled Rodger's gentle touch wiping her pussy and ass. Rodger noticed his wife's clumsiness and picked her up in one swoop, carrying her to the bedroom.

Susan lay on the bed waiting for her husband's thick cock as he slowly undressed in front of her. She looked at the chocolate, roses, and bottle of champagne that sat on her nightstand, coming to the conclusion that the rest of Rodger's romance package would have to wait until she was pleasured by him at least once. She giggled to herself thinking that he might have to pleasure her two or three more times after before they'd even get the chance to open up that bottle.

"I love you Susan," Rodger whispered into Susan's ear as he climbed on top of her and inserted his throbbing cock inside. "You are the most beautiful woman and wife that I ever could've asked for. Here's to the many years together that lie ahead of us."

The dream was entirely too real, too vivid for Susan to handle. Tears came rushing down her checks as she remembered her husband's last words. They had hoped to spend the rest of their lives together, at least until old age. There was always a joke about dying old together, sitting on rockers on their front porch in the middle of nowhere. That was their dream. Neither of them ever imagined Rodger was going to die almost exactly a year later.

Susan went to move her hand to wipe the streams of tears from her eyes when she realized Travis' were wrapped around her. The night before he had wiped away all of her fears, all of her sadness, unleashing the woman that once was. Now, after the terrible dream, Susan fell rock bottom again. A sickness rose inside her stomach, as she felt the familiar pangs of guilt settle underneath her skin. There was no way that she could be capable of moving on when she was having dreams of Rodger in her sleep. She had to get rid of Travis. She couldn't carry on like this, lying to him and lying to herself. She wasn't ready. Last night was yet another mistake.

Travis let out a sigh, opening his eyes at the beautiful woman who lay beside him. He tugged at her sides tightly with the length of his arms, pulling her in closer to him so he could plant a kiss on her forehead. He had thought that Susan was sleeping, but his surprise came swiftly when he saw the tears running down her face.

"Susan, what's wrong?" He asked, almost jumping out of bed.

Silence.

"Susan?" Travis asked again, embracing her cold body for a hug. "Susan, talk to me."

Susan lay still, unable to move. She felt as if she was being choked, unable to breathe, unable to let the words escape from her mouth. As she took in a large inhale, her ribs attempted to sputter let loose the words with her exhale, but the attempt fail. Instead, she broke down. Her cries sounding more like shrieks than anything.

Travis grabbed her lifeless body, trying to persuade vitality back into it once more. His heart broke into a thousand little pieces as Susan violently pushed him away.

"You have to go," she managed to say, almost pushing Travis off of the bed. "Last night was a mistake, a complete mistake. I can't keep doing this to myself, to you, or to Rodger. It isn't fair for any of us. I think it would be better if we never see each other again."

Travis sat on the edge of the bed, traumatized by the woman he had adored. The words that she had sputtered tore his soul into two. He finally had thought he had met his other half. He thought that last night had been the end to the guilt. He thought that now they would begin a future together, even if it was slow, he had thought it would be worth it.

"Susan," Travis began calmly. "Rodger, you're husband, is dead. I don't understand what it would be like to lose the person that you thought you'd spend the rest of your life with, but I know what it's like to grieve. You can't bring him back, Susan. Pushing me away from you is not going to bring him back."

"Travis, please just leave," Susan said sobbing. "Please don't make this harder on yourself."

Travis grabbed his clothes off of the floor and quickly dressed himself. Susan continued to cry, louder than she had been earlier. Travis thought to turn around from the door, to go back and comfort her, to try to make things work, but instead he continued walking. There was no point in trying to convince her. All that they had been doing was riding the waves of passion. Nothing of their relationship was common sense, only lustful desire that got the better of them. Travis closed the door behind him and never looked back.

As Susan sunk her feet further into the sands of the beach, she smiled at her realization that time truly does heal all wounds. It had been five months since

Rodger's passing and the beginning of her new life in California without him. Here, she was finally able to do what she loved without being looked down upon for being a simple high school English teacher. She had made friends almost instantly, and Ellen went from neighbor to best friend in a matter of months. A heavy pain still sat deep within Susan's heart, but it was becoming harder and harder to notice anymore. Rodger didn't want her to mourn for him for the rest of her life, and after some soul searching, Susan was finally beginning to find herself grieving for her late husband a lot less.

After making Travis leave her life at a time that was entirely way too inconvenient for her, Susan was finally left with an ability to think clearly without being persuaded by lust. There were times when she'd think about the passion that she and Travis had shared. There were times while speaking with Ellen in whom she wished she'd have the courage to ask about him, but she always avoided the thought. She locked the images of Travis' masculine hands caressing her body away from her mind, along with her husband's love. There was no way that Susan Hannold would be able to find the strength inside her to move on if she were going to be blindsided by emotions and lust.

Susan let out a heavy sigh and leaned back into the lounge chair. The sun was hot, causing her body to produce sweat that glistened against her now tanned skin. This time of year in New Hampshire would mean the changing color of the leaves and a cool breeze that caused its inhabitants a need to wear a sweater, but California was quite different. It was still warm. Warm enough to wear a bikini, a pair of shorts, and lay underneath the warm rays of the sunlight.

There was dryness inside of Susan's throat that made her reach across the sand and grab the Corona that she had ordered at the concession stand. Susan took in a large sip and closed her eyes, hearing no other sound other than the waves of the ocean cracking against the beach. She heard no other sounds, that is, until she heard strong footsteps nearing behind her. She leaned back against the chair again, considering that the footsteps were more than likely those of a child who would soon be kicking wet sand against her parched body.

"Mind if I take a seat next to you?" asked a man with a familiar voice.

Susan's body froze, knowing very well who the familiar voice reminded her of. Without looking at the figure of the man whom was speaking, or even thinking for that matter, Susan quickly replied with an answer.

"Yes."

Susan still kept her eyes closed, her head still firmly pressed against the lounger. She listened clearly without watching, using her ears to made a sound judgment of what the man was doing rather than her eyes. She could tell by the sounds that were overcoming her senses that the man had pulled out a blanket and laid it next her lounger. The thud, Susan was sure, was that of him sitting down taking a seat next to her. Her eyes may have been closed, but she could feel that his eyes were staring at her. They were smiling, happy with the reflection that they were taking in.

The man inhaled deeply, not knowing where to start.

"How are you doing Susan?" the man asked. "It's been some time since we've last seen each other."

Susan took another sip of her Corona, not showing much emotion as she began to speak.

"Well," she began. "I've been well. The school year started last month. I finally feel like I'm starting to fit in with the students. I'm starting to feel like I'm fitting in with California, as if I belong here. It's funny that I've spent much of my life living on the East Coast, miserable, when the West Coast truly was the place where I belonged."

Travis sat in silence, pondering where he should begin. As much as he enjoyed seeing the woman whom he hadn't been able to forget these last few months, he couldn't help but feel annoyed that she wouldn't even look at him. The sweat glistening down Susan's chest down onto her large breasts was making Travis hard. He quickly readjusted his excited member, still keeping his focus on the beautifully sculpted neckline that was Susan's.

"Sometimes, the funny thing about life," Travis began, nervously. "Is that the thing we need the most seems unobtainable. You were miserable in New Hampshire and knew it, but stayed there anyways. Really, you probably knew that if you used the courage to move out of the location that you would fill your void with happiness. We push away ideas that are healing because we're afraid of the changes that we will have to make. I'm glad that you have found your courage. That's what I've admired about you all along. You are one damn strong woman, Susan."

Susan blushed behind the large sunglasses that she wore and sat up in the chair. She wanted to remove the shades and look into Travis' eyes, but he was right. Sometimes, she especially, pushed away ideas that were healing because she was afraid of the changes that they would make. Travis was one of them. She pushed away a man that adored her because she was afraid of what was to come of the relationship. It wasn't that Rodger had died, it wasn't the guilt even. It was the fear that Travis created inside of her, a fear of experiencing love with a person that wasn't Rodger, a fear of ever loving again. To love again meant Susan loving herself, and Susan, after a decade of self-hate, wasn't sure on how to do that.

"I'm sorry that I made you leave," Susan blurted out. "I'm sorry that I pushed you away Travis. I shouldn't have, but I was scared."

"Don't apologize to me" Travis insisted, taking Susan's hand into his. "I should've known better. Here you were still mourning your husband's loss, and all I could think about is how much I wanted you. If I were smart, I would've taken things much slower. I would've known that you needed time."

Susan pulled the shades off her face, exposing her rosy cheeks that had been given color from her embarrassment. She looked deeply into Travis' eyes, eyes that apparently still yearned for her.

"I haven't stopped thinking about you Travis," Susan began. "I've pushed you away because I needed to in order to survive. I needed to find my own strength, my own courage, my own place in this world again. But I haven't ever stopped thinking about you. There's a magic that we had shared. I know that it is too late now, but..."

Travis broke Susan's sentence with a kiss. His thick, juicy lips plummeted against her own. She felt heat rise within her body as she playfully licked his lips in return. All of this time, she had been running away from the man who had helped her turn into the woman that she was becoming. She did not want to spend the rest of her life in regret. She wanted Travis more than she had ever wanted anything before.

Hungry moans escaped from their mouths as Susan and Travis continued pleasuring each other with their tongues. Susan could feel her nipples harden inside of her bikini top. Their relationship had always ended in sex, something that Susan had felt wrong about, but this time, she knew that wanting to feel Travis inside of her was one of the best desires she had felt in a long time.

Susan broke free from the kiss, looking deeply into Travis' eyes. She moved her attention across the vacant beach, searching for a passerby who might have found their public display of affection to be too much to be seen by the general public. She wanted Travis, and she wanted him now, but the risk of being found on the beach while making love to him made Susan wary. A wild idea sprang into her mind.

"Would you be interested in going for a short walk?" Susan asked, while licking her lips. "I know a quiet spot further down the beach. We could continue this without running into the risk of a voyeur."

"Sure," Travis quickly responded, jumping up to his feet and grabbing the blanket up from underneath him.

Susan giggled, grabbing Travis by the hand and pulling him across the sand. She finally felt free, no longer a prisoner of her past or of her own emotions. A quarter mile down the beach, Susan led Travis to the supreme oasis that waited them. Susan opened up the brush, presenting the chunk of beach that was hidden behind the trees. Travis laid down the blanket and made himself comfortable against its fabric. Susan took a seat next to him. She was surprised at the force Travis used to pull her down closer to him. She excitedly locked her lips against his, sealing her mouth with his for a kiss.

Travis brushed Susan's hair away from her face. Her playful tongue researching his mouth was making his member stiffen out from his swim trunks. Susan giggled at the head of his cock as it found its freedom from his shorts. Knowing that she was making the man yearn for her was making her wet with desire. Travis lightly pushed Susan's body across the blanket. He smiled down at the gorgeous woman below him.

"You're so beautiful," he whispered into

Susan's ear. "I couldn't stop thinking about you all of this time."

Susan leaned her head back and smiled, feeling the sensation of Travis' tongue roam across her neck. She never wanted to let him go again either, but most of all, she didn't want to feel this sensation stop. Her body was now drenched in the heat of their lovemaking rather than that of the sun. Although the place she had led him was private, knowing the probability of someone finding them and catching them in the act was an incredible turn on. Susan could feel her pussy get wet just by thinking about it.

Travis led his tongue down to Susan's chest and stopped at her breasts. He lifted his head up from her skin, smiling at her as he unleashed her large breasts from the bathing suit top. Her hardened nipples smiled back at him, giving him the permission to perform on them. He wildly licked and sucked at her nipples, the assault on them making Susan's body rise up off of the ground. She stuck her hands out reaching for Travis' dick, but his member was too far out of her reach. She unbuttoned the button on her shorts instead, reaching her hand down to spread her pussy lips and then inserting her excited finger deep inside. She pushed in and out of her warm, slippery hole. Travis continued to tease at her nipples, as he reached down to pull out his dick from his shorts.

"I want you inside of me," Susan whispered into Travis' ear. "I want you inside of me and I never want to ever let you go. I love you, Travis."

Travis viewed Susan's plain face, seeing the lust for him that poured out from her eyes. She had just whispered the words right out of his mouth.

"I love you too, Susan Hannold," he said, as he inserted himself inside of her. "I love you and I promise to never let you go."

5 AWAKENING WATERS

Time seems to go on forever when you are watching for the clock hands to turn to a number that you've been waiting for. At least Sophia felt that way, sitting in her office, signing the documents piled in front of her, and trying to ignore those atrocious hands. Normally, she liked this job. Normally, she felt like there wasn't enough time to keep performing. When the clock would hit five, Sophia would pretend not to notice, finishing up the paper stacks until they were obsolete. She became the joke around the office.

"Where's Dr. Lewis?" they would ask. "Still sitting around in her office? Doesn't she have a home to go to, one that doesn't resemble Good Night Moon?"

Sophia looked up from the paperwork before her and viewed the depictions of bunnies from the story painted onto the wall and smiled. She loved this place, every aspect of it, from the décor to the patients. She loved working with children, observing the courage that so many of them had. Courage, so natural, something the average adult could only wish they still could feel. She loved these tiny little faces that beamed up at her with joy when she told them they we're going to be okay. They believed her. They only held her below their parents or God as the most trustworthy, heroic person on the face of the universe. To these children, Sophia Lewis was a hero. To these children, Sophia Lewis was special – if only other people thought that way.

Sophia felt quite the opposite of special to her husband Damien. They had only been married for three months now, and the fire already seemed to burn out. Who was Sophia kidding though? There really wasn't much of a fire before they got married. She stuck with Damien those two years prior only because she didn't want to have to bother going through the process of dating again. He was an okay man, really, an average man who was very handsome at least. April seemed to like him, so that was good enough for Sophia. April was so polished, so put together, so in the now. How she and Sophia remained friends after all of these years still surprised Sophia, but she loved her. She was the sister Sophia never had, and if she said Damien Lewis was a great guy, she might as well marry the man. April always had Sophia's best interest in heart.

Sophia moved her eyes onto the clock. She really had been trying to avoid it, telling herself that her anticipation was childish, but she couldn't help but to feel excited to leave early from work and take the first real vacation she had taken in what seemed like years. The fire may have lacked in Sophia and Damien's marriage, but tonight she was going to make it up to him. She knew she was to blame for most of it, turning Damien down every chance she got and choosing to be more involved with her work than with him. Damien might not have been the man of her dreams, but Sophia was realizing that they made a pact to stay together forever, and she was not doing her part to make that stay a happy one. Tonight she was going to cook that man the meal of his life and make real some of his dirtiest fantasies for dessert. She was going to please her man tonight - she owed it to him. Not just because she had been cold to his affection for months now, but also because April and her were going to go on a girls-only vacation to the island of Martinique the next day. Sophia couldn't bear the thought of leaving her man empty handed while she enjoyed the benefits of the island sun without him. He deserved a night of romance with her, he deserved her affection.

Sophia walked into her apartment, with brown bags of groceries in her hand, and took a whiff of the air. Her lavender candle was burning, which she found odd being that Damien never lit candles in their home, at least not ever in her presence. She wanted to call out his name and ask him about it when she didn't see him in the living room, but figured she'd wait. He probably laid down for a nap anyways, not knowing that she was leaving work early that day, so Sophia figured she'd head to the kitchen and start dinner before waking him up and ruining the surprise just to ask about a silly candle burning.

Her body came to a complete freeze though when she passed the bedroom and heard noises coming out from inside. She heard the moans of a woman, not experiencing pain, but obviously pleasure. Sophia stood there in shock. What the hell was going on here? Blame filled her mind as she realized that she and Damien hadn't even engaged in sex since their wedding night. What type of wife was she being to him? Here they are a young, healthy, newly married couple, and she hasn't even attempted to have sex with her husband at all. Sophia felt down right terrible, as she came to conclusion that poor Damien had to fill his needs somehow. He was obviously watching porn in order to take care of his needs, since his pitiful wife refused to please him.

Sophia figured she'd let the man finish the deed and make dinner anyways. She was going to give him the best dessert that he had ever eaten that night, so it would be best if he got off beforehand. That way he'd be able to last the hours that Sophia had planned to seduce him. She licked her lips a little, the thought of her man behind the door with his hands bouncing up and down on his cock was making her horny.

"Fuck dinner!" she thought while grabbing the doorknob. "What a surprise it will be when Damien finds I came home early to suck his cock."

She fumbled a little with the groceries, thinking to put them down first before entering the room, but changing her mind when she realized she had chocolate syrup and whipped cream in one of the bags. She planned to use them later on Damien's body for dessert, but since they were going to have dessert a little earlier than expected, she needed them to top her confection.

A sly smile appeared on Sophia's face, thinking about how naughty things were going to be once she opened that bedroom door. She had never done anything like this for Damien, or any other man for that matter; the thought of this made her feel powerful and incredibly turned on. But once Sophia opened the door, all of her erotic feelings flew out it, as she stood there watching Damien's cock ram in and out of April's pussy from behind.

Neither Damien nor April noticed the voyeur watching their act from behind them. They continued moaning in and out of their own ecstasy, April screaming one last "Oh my God!" and then unleashing her fluids onto her best friend's husband's dick. Damien looked down and saw April's juices cover his stiffened member and lost it. He pulled out quickly and shot his jizz all over her ass.

Standing up, Damien looked down at April and said, "Damn, babe, that's some of the best pussy I ever had! Thank you."

April smiled, trying to snap the enclosures of her bra together and turned around to see her best friend standing there in astonishment. Fear released through her body, not knowing what Sophia was going to do to her. She knew that her deceit and betrayal to her friend was wrong, but she wanted Damien since she first met him. She tried to respect their relationship, not to get involved, but after Damien confided in her a few weeks ago asking if Sophia was cheating on him because she wasn't giving him any, she knew that she had to have her way with him. She wasn't going to let this hot piece of meat get away from her, not when his own wife didn't care to fuck him. She swore she only meant to fuck him once. She just wanted to see what he was like. She never planned to keep fucking him every day when Sophia was away at work. She never meant to ever hurt her best friend. She just thought she'd never find out.

The bags of groceries dropped onto the floor, the can of whipped cream exploding onto the carpet and catching the attention of Damien who was now turned around staring at his wife's horrified face. Sophia just stood in shock, unable to move. She knew that she had been a terrible wife to Damien; she already felt guilty about that. She'd understand him wanting to cheat on her, but with her, with April?

"What the fuck is going on here?!" screamed Sophia, feet still frozen to the ground. "You're sleeping with my best friend?! What the fuck is wrong with you April?! How could you hurt me like this?!"

Damien's mouth now resembled that of a capital O. A million thoughts raced throughout his mind, none of which holding a viable excuse for Sophia. He never truly wanted April. Sure, they flirted a little from time to time, mostly on her part, but he never planned to sleep with her. She may have been sexy and she may of dressed trashy and caught the eyes of most men she walked by, but Damien wasn't into that type of girl. He knew that no man could turn a whore into a housewife, at least that's what he told himself.

He wanted a good woman, a woman he was proud to display to his family. Sophia was that kind of woman; Sophia was sexy in that right. It just was that over a year had gone by since she truly seemed interested in him; even on their wedding night, making love to her was like making love to a corpse. No matter the romance that he tried to create or the passion he tried to ignite, Sophia showed no interest. She was always so focused on her work, so cold to him.

He thought to himself in split seconds, while reviewing the eyes of his now morose wife, how this affair all really happened. He just wanted to know if Sophia was cheating on him, that was all, truly. His wife was hardly ever home anymore. He thought for sure that she had met somebody at the office, someone more attractive, and someone more successful than him. If anybody might know if his wife was cheating, it would've been April and that's why he sought her out in the first place. He never expected her to come on to him. In normal circumstances, that is if his wife actually had shown interest in him, he would've turned her down. But she looked just too damn hot in that black tube dress that day, that dress that perfectly showcased her giant bosoms and perfect round ass. He hadn't been laid in so long that his dick was almost dying to be touched. He couldn't help it, but he never planned on it to happen again afterward. April just kept showing up at the apartment while Sophia was at work, each time wearing something entirely way too revealing. She was a seductress and he just couldn't say no to her.

Today was going to be different. At least that's what Damien originally thought. He invited April over because he planned now was the perfect timing to stop this madness. April and his wife were going to go to Martinique the next day, which would be time away from the temptress so he could clear his thoughts and start over. He figured their vacation would be the end to the affair and the beginning to him and his wife's new direction. He planned to tell her that he was done. He planned to tell her that this wasn't right. But when April showed up in a trench coat with nothing on underneath, he found himself unable to control his urges once more. But what did it matter at this point? How could he explain all of this to her wife and gain her sympathy? The only way he could was by telling her the truth.

"It's not what it looks like, Sophia," Damien finally said, lungs barely able to process the stale air in the room.

"It's not?!" questioned Sophia, still yelling at

the two suspects in front of her. "Then why does it look like this? Why did I walk into our bedroom to find you fucking my best friend? I've seen the two of you release with each other. I heard what you said to her at the end. I find your answer kind of funny, Damien, since from what I've seen is exactly what it looks like. It looked like two of my favorite, most trustworthy people in the world have wronged me, have hurt me. I know that I've been a shitty wife Damien, but this was uncalled for. I want the two of you the fuck out of my house, now!"

April finally came unglued from the floor and started walking toward Sophia.

"Soph...honey..." she started, tears beginning to stream down her cheeks. "We never meant to hurt you, I swear!"

Fire burned inside of Sophia's body, an anger unleashing that a woman of her nature had never felt before. Her arm jolted and as April walked toward her attempting to embrace her with a hug, Sophia reached out her hand and slapped her hard across her face, leaving a stinging sensation in the palm of her hand.

"Our friendship is over, April," said Sophia, looking at the shock in her ex-best friend's face. "You are the dumbest bitch I know. We were friends since we drew on the cement with sidewalk chalk, and because of that, I have always loved you and remained close. When everybody else was talking shit on you, about how much of a whore you were, I stood beside you. I backed you up. I made excuses for you, saying that that's just how you were – a free spirit, a fun-loving girl. But I always knew the truth, April. I always knew you were just a dirty slut. I just never knew how much of a slut you really were."

"I want the both of you out of here, now!" Sophia continued, looking at the pitiful faces before her and catching her breath.

"But...Soph...baby..." Damien pleaded. "Where am I going to go?"

Sophia let out an evil laugh while walking over to the pile of Damien's clothes on the floor.

"You wanted to fuck April?" questioned Sophia as she threw the mass toward her husband. "Well you can fuck her all you want now. Go stay with that whore; fuck her all night long for all that I care. Just get the fuck out of here Damien. I want the both of you the fuck out of here now!"

"But...but..." April and Damien stammered.

"NOW!" exclaimed Sophia, flames burning in her eyes.

The apartment seemed so empty now with Damien gone. What began as a day that was planned to become one of the best days of Sophia's life instantly became ruined with betrayal and deceit.

"Happy 30th birthday," said Sophia grimly to herself. "What an amazing decade this one will be."

She slumped down onto the sectional sofa, rivers streaming down her cheeks. This was not something she ever expected to find. She just never thought that the two people she loved would hurt her like this. Who else did she have now? She lost her parents when she was young, and although she did have a few friends, mostly from work, she had no one to truly turn to.

Perhaps she stayed with a man she barely loved anymore and a friend who turned into the biggest whore on Earth because she simply had no one else, she thought to herself. She spent years of her life yearning for parents who weren't there, but always had April. She later on had Damien to turn to, even if it meant he was there more to keep her company rather than excited. At least he was there; at least she wasn't lonely with him lying beside her each night. Being married to Damien meant not having an empty apartment to come home to, but now that was exactly what she had. The apartment was not the only empty thing though, Sophia was feeling empty inside.

If only, she thought, if only she appreciated Damien a little more. She may not have felt any lust for the man, but she could've at least given him affection for his friendship. Maybe not even sex, just a cuddle, just a night out, and just a night that meant coming home early and acting like he mattered to her.

She leaned down over her knees, cupping her head into the palms of her hands. Her head hurt, thoughts spinning out of control. "What to do now?" she thought. What the hell am I going to do without them?

Sophia's eyes glanced down at the coffee

table in front of her. Her passport, plane tickets, and travel guides sat there looking back up at her. Martinique, that's what Sophia was going to do. She may have lost the only two people she had in this world, but she still had a trip planned to celebrate her birthday. April obviously wasn't going to accompany her on the trip anymore, but she still had reservations to take up. She still had a beautiful island awaiting her.

Sophia looked at the time she had scheduled to board the plane headed for the island the next day – 6 a.m. She thought to herself that she had better get some sleep. She had already packed her bags the night before, so she could get some well-deserved rest for the night, forgetting about the two people who wronged her and waking up renewed in the morning. She grabbed her cell phone out of her front pocket, ignoring the missed calls that she had from April and Damien, and shut off the device.

"Good riddance," she thought to herself, now laying her head onto a pillow. "I don't need either of you after all."

What would've seemed like an exciting plane ride turned into a tormenting one for Sophia. She had no one to talk to, just a vacant seat that sat beside her where April would've been. Having that empty seat next to her made her have to think about April, thoughts that she wished she could've avoided. Still, Sophia felt much different today. She felt powerful and strong. She felt determined. She may have been a crappy wife to a man that she truly hadn't loved in some time, but she wasn't to blame for his cheating. He could've talked to her about things; he could've voiced his loneliness. And April? She didn't have to go and spread her legs all over her husband. She didn't have to be the whore that she was. She chose to be a nymphomaniac. She chose to have no respect. Sophia finally decided that she wasn't at fault for any of this. They were and she was done with each of them, for good.

April and Sophia spent months looking at different brochures and online sources regarding the island, all of which looked beautiful and all of which made the place look phenomenal, but once getting off the plane and seeing her surroundings, Sophia was finally able to understand how breathtaking the beauty of this island truly was. White sands covered the beaches with crystal clear waters that splashed up against them. From the car ride to the resort, Sophia found that the island was covered with luscious, tropical rain forests. There were plantations spread across the land, all of which carried their own whimsical island charm. Quaint towns sat on top of streets, full of diverse culture and architecture both modern and old. There was so much to take in regarding this place. Sophia just couldn't wait to get to the resort and start her stay.

It was a rather hot and humid day, but that wasn't why Sophia felt the strong urge for a drink. What better way to unwind, relax, and forget about all of her troubles back home than to have a nice glass of wine? Sophia quickly unpacked her bags and threw on a light summer dress. Hell, she needed this drink.

Smiling, happy faces of all colors and creeds greeted Sophia as she made her way down to the hotel's bar. She took the lone, empty seat at the oval-shaped bar and greeted the attractive bartender standing in the middle of it.

"A Riesling, please," she asked politely.

"Sure thing, doll," replied the bartender.

Sophia drank the glass of wine as if it were the only liquid she had seen in days. The drink that followed went down even smoother. She may have come to the island alone, without the presence of the woman who destroyed her life, but while at the bar, she had more company than she had ever had with April.

A group of five women lined the seats beside the one Sophia sat in, all of which were here at Martinique on a girl's vacation. All of them were married, mostly with children, and came to the island just looking for some relaxation, just looking for a little bit of fun on their own, without their families. They warmed up to Sophia quickly and within a few minutes were laughing and talking together as if they had known each other all of their lives. Sophia thought to tell them about the disaster that she had left home, but decided against it. She wanted to enjoy this trip and forget about the scenario that now disgusted her more than anything. Sharing in some much needed girl talk with these women was just the right medicine.

"He's looking at you," whispered the brown-haired woman sitting next to Sophia.

"Who?" laughed Sophia, taking her last gulp of wine.

"The man across from you, on the other side of the bar," the woman responded. "He's been watching you since you've entered the room, only to occasionally look away. It's like his eyes are glued or something."

Sophia called for the bartender, she needed another refill on her drink, but really, she needed someone to slightly block her view so she could inspect her admirer. The bartender took her order and turned around to pour the concoction into a new glass, giving Sophia the perfect chance to glance toward the man. Her heart skipped a million beats when she saw his face. He was beautiful, not at all what Sophia had expected. She thought someone who would look at her obsessively like this would resemble someone who was aged, had poor looks, and perhaps overweight even, but this man was the most gorgeous man she had ever laid eyes on. He had short, dark black hair, with well-chiseled features. His facial structure so perfectly sculpted, and his face reminded Sophia of a sculpture that only the gods could themselves create. His deep brown mysterious eyes flashed a smile into Sophia's, making her blush and look away once the bartender returned with her drink.

"You should talk to him," the brunette persisted. "Honey, he's gorgeous!"

"I'm not interested," Sophia responded, taking a fresh sip of her drink.

"Oh, are you married?" asked the woman suspiciously, looking into Sophia's eyes.

"Something of the sort," Sophia responded dimly, remembering Damien in the act of having sex her best friend.

"Well that's a damn shame," said the brunette who now had a frown on her face.

Sophia laughed.

"Why don't you go after him?" she teased.

"Oh, honey…" replied the older woman. "I'm a married woman. I came to this island to have fun, but not to cheat on my husband. Besides, he's interested in you anyways."

Sophia took another gulp of her drink, this time finishing its remains. She could feel the man's eyes examining her from across the bar and was starting to feel uncomfortable. He may have been the sexiest piece of ass she had seen since coming onto the island, if not even in her lifetime, but she didn't come to Martinique to have an affair. She didn't want to end up sleeping with a man who would be nothing but sex during her vacation anyways. Her heart always got too involved in her relationships. She just never was one of those women to have one-night stands. Even though Damien wronged her, she still felt guilty. She couldn't cheat on her husband, if that was what he even was still, even if he deserved it.

Sophia got up and quickly excused herself from the group of women. She made plans to meet with the women again while on her stay on the island. She took down their room numbers and slowly walked away. She took one last look before leaving the room and saw the handsome patron eyeing her every step as she exited.

"Damn it!" she thought to herself. "He

might have been worth the risk."

The whole way up to her room, Sophia couldn't stop thinking about the man who was looking at her. He was so dreamy; she couldn't help but to think what he might have looked like naked, his lips pressing against hers. She swiped her key card inside the slot on the door. Once it clicked open, she drunkenly collapsed onto the bed. Perhaps she had a bit much to drink.

She lay for a while on the bed, thinking of Damien. Why did she still feel attached to a man that was unfaithful to her? Anger filled her veins, still remembering the scene that played out before her the day before. God damn it, Sophia! You never truly loved him in the first place.

The man at the bar popped into her head once more. Was he really looking at her? He could've been a Calvin Klein model. He was that perfect. She envisioned what would've happened if she took up the brunette's offer at the bar to go up and talk to him. Would they kiss? Would it lead to so much more? She thought of what he would've looked like underneath the shirt that tightly clenched his arms and chest. He had to have been ripped, with a six-pack and all. Her daydream about a complete stranger came as a surprise to Sophia when she realized that it was turning her on. She started to think what he would look like beneath those perfected abs, rock hard, waiting for her. Her mouth began to water, and she realized that maybe she needed a shower to break her out of his spell. Maybe she just needed to sober up a little in order to think straight.

Sophia grabbed her silk camisole and boy shorts and headed toward the shower, still feeling a heat inside her panties. The pressure of the shower head was so invigorating, making Sophia moan as her muscles began to relax. She envisioned the man massaging her shoulders completely nude behind her, rather than the showerhead performing all the work. He worked his hands slowly down her bare back stopping before he reached her ass. Sophia let out another moan. She wasn't sure if it was from the pressure of the water or the thoughts that began to follow.

She felt the man firmly placing both of his hands onto her buttocks, massaging each one and then lowering himself to his knees. He slowly opened each lip of her pussy with his fingers, placing his tongue inside her wet cunt beneath her. He was licking back and forth up her slippery cunt when Sophia realized she couldn't control her visualizations anymore. She had to get off. She had to masturbate. The thought of this man was just making her way too hot, unable to control her body's natural response. She slid her finger across her hardened clit and then into her gaping hole, pressing it harder and faster each time she entered. His tongue felt so good, roughly penetrating her pussy; she was going to cum her hot juices all over his face.

"Cum for me, baby," she heard him say. "I

want you to cum all over my face."

Sophia bounced up and down on the two fingers that she had now inserted into herself, feeling a rush come over her body. Tiny explosions rippled inside her as she let out a loud moan for all of the hotel's residents to hear.

"Oh I'm going to come for you, baby," she said screaming, feeling her own juices flood against her fingers.

She washed her fingers underneath the warm water, feeling a smile that lit her face side to side. She may not have had passionate sex with Damien in some time now, but she sure as hell knew how to pleasure herself. She finished washing up, slipping into the camiset once dried. She figured she'd stay in the rest of the night, drink some of the bottled wine that the hotel provided for her, and catch some TV. But her idea for a quiet night in seemed so bland once she found a mysterious note that had been slipped underneath her door while showering.

"Come have dinner with me tonight gorgeous," the note read. "Meet me at the port at 8:30. I will be waiting for you."

Sophia poured herself a tall glass of wine. She was going to need it, embarking on a journey she once would never have taken, but something about this note was dangerous. She didn't know who it was from, the man at the bar perhaps. Either way, with the turn of events that had been facing her, danger seemed kind of sexy. Sophia stood in front of the mirror, admiring how hot she looked in the low cut dress she put on for the night's occasion. Whoever was going to meet her tonight, she could guarantee would be in for a big surprise. Sophia wasn't going to be wearing any underwear.

While walking down toward the port, Sophia passed clusters of happy couples holding hands. Was what she was planning on doing wrong? Guilt still consumed her body. She was still married to Damien after all, but the excitement of meeting a mysterious man for dinner was such a big turn on, considering that it might just be the man she had pleasured herself to about an hour ago.

She could see the outline of a tall, dark man standing next to a boat at the port, but the sun's evening rays were blocking the fine details of his looks. Fear raced through her body, making her heart pound heavily in her chest. This whole time the thought never crossed Sophia's mind that maybe this man meant ill will toward her, until now, until she was almost standing right in front of him. It was too late to turn back; the man had already spotted her and was headed her direction.

"You're late," he said with a smile, resembling the man from the bar.

"Yeah, sorry about that," Sophia replied, trying to ignore the butterflies in her stomach once she realized who he was. "I wasn't sure at first if I should meet you."

"That's understandable," he said, still smiling into Sophia's eyes. "I wasn't sure if you would come. This has been the first time I ever had the audacity to do something like this."

"That makes two of us," Sophia quickly responded, trying to mentally tell the butterflies in her stomach to calm down.

The man laughed.

"I'm Andre by the way," he said, pulling out his hand so Sophia could shake it. "I saw you at the bar today and wanted to talk to you, but must admit I was too shy at the time."

"It's nice to meet you, Andre," said Sophia as she shook his hand, starting to blush.

She wanted to melt away into his arms. French, she could tell by his accent that he was French. Andre was already the hottest man she had ever laid eyes on, but he was French too? Sophia almost had to pinch herself so that she could be sure that she wasn't dreaming.

"I'm Sophia." She said, doing a little curtsey. "I'm glad that you didn't forget me then."

"Forget you?" Andre asked, while watching her pale complexion turn red. "I tried Sophia, but I couldn't stop thinking about you."

Sophia was still smiling, revealing a small dimple in the crease of her cheek. The two stood in an awkward silence, staring blankly at each other.

"Well, to dinner then?" questioned Andre, pointing toward the direction of his boathouse. "I hope you like seafood, as that is the main course that I have planned. Although I will be happy to provide you with a vegetarian option or a nice cut of beef"

"No, seafood is absolutely fine Andre," Sophia responded. "Please tell me you didn't go through much trouble in order to entertain just me."

Andre laughed, trying to keep his eyes on Sophia's alluring, dark brown eyes rather than her exceptionally large breasts.

"Well I am a chef, Sophia," Andre answered. "Besides, no food would be too much trouble if it meant entertaining you."

Sophia ran her hand up to her face and felt her now flaming cheeks. This man was perfect, almost a dream come true. She followed behind him as he walked onto the boathouse, her jaw dropping in awe once viewing how luxurious it was inside. An exquisite, white sectional sofa lined the walls of the living room area and a white and black mod coffee table sitting before it. Sophia's eyes drew onto the direction of the large flat screen hanging on the wall across from the seating arrangement. Andre was obviously one loaded chef.

"Come...Come..." Andre said to Sophia, who was standing in the middle of his living room, inspecting it with astonishment. "Dinner is ready."

Sophia, embarrassed, quickly walked toward the dining area. A rounded glass table sat in the middle of it, decorated with square, white plates and a glass centerpiece containing a white orchid surrounded by rocks. Sophia took a seat in one of the cushiony chairs Andre had used against the glass table. Her stomach roared as she took whiffs at the deliciousness circulating through the air. Andre wasn't lying, by the smell of the food cooking, it was clear the man was a chef.

"Riesling?" he asked, getting prepared to

pour the contents of the bottle into the glass sitting in front of Sophia.

"Yes, please," Sophia responded, rising the glass for the bottle's pour. "Riesling is my favorite."

"I could tell from the way you were drinking it at the bar," said Andre chuckling and then turning around to grab a pan off of the stove.

"Tonight's feast," he began, while filling Sophia's plate with bits of everything. "Will include Caribbean bass with a honey nutmeg sauce, roasted red potatoes, pan tossed kale, and a sweet potato soufflé."

Sophia eyed the gorgeousness of the presentation.

"This looks wonderful, Andre," she said. "Absolutely wonderful!"

Andre sat down across from Sophia with a plate of his own. The two laughed and engaged in small talk while eating; Andre occasionally found himself distracted by Sophia's lips as she took in bites of food. He learned that she was from the United States and was touring the island of Martinique alone. He wondered if that was honestly the truth as she was way too beautiful, at least in his eyes, not to have a partner.

"I want to thank you for coming out tonight," Andre said, finishing the last bite he was going to take of the meal. "It truly has been a marvelous time."

"Well thank you for inviting me," Sophia replied. "The meal was spectacular and I've enjoyed your company very much."

"I've made dessert," Andre said, pleased that he was showing such a gorgeous woman a good time. "How about another glass of Riesling while we share my banana torte on the couch together?"

"Banana torte?" questioned Sophia, sultriness in her tone. "I'm yours."

Andre beamed at her, watching Sophia pour more Riesling into each of their glasses. Her voracious ass jiggled back at him, as she walked toward the couch, making him have to mentally tell his hardened member to tone it down, to take it slow.

Sophia hadn't said anything since sitting down on the couch; she just sat quietly and sipped her wine, watching the handsome French man cut slivers from the torte. She didn't have much appetite for it, not because she wasn't still hungry or because it didn't seem appealing, but because Sophia was starting to feel an appetite for something more sensual. Andre walked toward her, two dessert plates in hand, handing one to Sophia. She played around a little with the torte, taking small bites with her fingers. Andre watched her, worried that perhaps she didn't like it.

"Do you not like it?" Andre asked, taking a sip of wine after to hide his worry.

"It's not that I don't like it," Sophia slowly responded, knowing what she was going to say next was going to be entirely out of character. "The banana torte is quite tasty Andre, but I think I'd rather have you in my mouth for dessert instead."

202

The sound of Andre's gulp echoed in the room.

"Sure!" he responded in amazement, almost in a state of shock from her forwardness.

Sophie sat down her plate and leaned toward Andre, taking his plate from his frozen hands. She giggled as she jumped onto his lap and looked into his wild eyes.

"You're so handsome, Andre," she whispered.

"And you, Sophia, are the most beautiful woman that I have ever met."

Sophia pressed her hips into the indent of his jeans. He was hard as a rock and Sophia couldn't wait to feel it inside her. They embraced into a kiss, tongues swirling into each other's mouths. Sophia could hear Andre moaning underneath his breath, making her even hornier. She rocked back and forth on his cloth-covered cock, moaning in its anticipation. Andre reached down so he could unleash his hard member but found his jeans were soaked with Sophia's fluids. He moved his hand instead toward Sophia's crotch, finding the surprise of warm pussy lips not covered by any underwear touching his hand. Andre let out a moan as he bit playfully on the lips that were ravishing his; Sophia moaned in return. He circled her clit with his fingers feeling Sophia's juices flow onto his hands. God, she was wet!

Sophia sucked hard on Andre's tongue, teasing him while exploring it as she knew he'd like her to explore his dick. His fingers felt so right playing with her the way he was, much better than the masturbation session she had given herself earlier. The entire dinner, Andre had teased her senses by wearing a tank top showcasing perfectly fit muscles underneath. Sophia wanted so badly to see the package without clothes. She tore at his shirt, roughly pulling it over his head like an animal. A gorgeous chest lay in front of her with hardened nipples waiting to be sucked. She slid her tongue down the creases of his neck, teasing him to his collarbone with her mouth. She scrunched down and licked his erect nipples up and down, and she became increased with wetness as she listened to the sounds of Andre's ecstasy.

Sophia's tongue flicking at his nipples was almost enough to make Andre explode. He now was finger fucking Sophia's pussy with two of his fingers. She gyrated up and down on them, increasing her pleasure. She felt like she was going to cum all over his hand and decided she wanted to save her grand finale for his cock. She abruptly got off of him and started unbuttoning his jeans, pulling out a perfectly sculpted 8-inch penis. Her eyes widened as she lustfully looked at the thick head of his swollen member. She leaned over it and playfully licked it with her tongue. Teasingly she licked up and down its shaft until her mouth enclosed all around it, taking all eight of its inches head on. She bobbed up and down on it, licking its sides, experiencing a few times in which she thought Andre was going to explode.

"Sit on my dick, babe," he said, gently lifting her head off his cock. "I want to feel that wet pussy of yours."

Sophia got off her knees and sat on top of his dick, her eyes glued to his. She let out a thunderous moan as her pussy engulfed each inch of him, until finally reaching all eight. Andre grabbed the bottom of her ass cheeks and bounced her up and down on his thick shaft. Watching the look on Sophia's face as she was being penetrated was making him want to cum inside of her.

"Oh God...!" Sophia moaned, her hand now feverishly playing with her clit. "I'm going to cum!"

Sophia felt the explosion of juices drizzle down his cock as her muscles released their tension. She felt listless as Andre continued to bounce her up and down on his cock, feeling his cock begin to stiffen against her now contracting muscles. She moaned in unison with him as she felt his hot squirt drizzle out of her vagina back onto his cock. The two fell into each other, letting out their final moans and finishing with a sensual kiss.

Andre looked into Sophia's eyes.

"Whew!" he said, wiping sweat from his brows. "That was awesome."

"Mmmmm," Sophia responded, licking his lip one last time.

She could barely breathe.

Even though Sophia had paid for an extravagant hotel room, which now was empty, she found the comfort of Andre's bed to be the relaxation she had thoroughly hoped for. They lied on the fluffy down feather mattress for a while talking about food, Paris, and how great their sex was. Sophia learned during their conversation that Andre was born and raised in France to an aristocrat family. He attended one of the top French culinary schools in the country and learned to master the presentation and taste of food. As a boy, he had spent many summers at his family's vacation home on the island of Martinique and fell in love with the country and its diverse culture. Being that owning a restaurant in Paris meant a lot of world-renowned competition, Andre decided to move to Martinique and start his restaurant on the island instead.

Sophia was fascinated by the man. His life seemed much more exciting compared to the people she had known back home. She liked the fact that he seemed interested in her and what she did. She liked that he adored the passion she held for treating disease-stricken children. He called her a hero and made Sophia feel special. Damien never seemed interested in Sophia's work; if anything, he always seemed annoyed by the fact that Sophia had such a passion for children. Damien always said he wasn't ready for children and that's why they never tried to have any, but Sophia knew deep down inside that Damien simply didn't want any.

Looking at the hunk of attractive man lying beside her, Sophia pushed the reminders of Damien out of her mind. She finally had met her prince charming; she wasn't going to waste the moments she shared with him thinking about the man who wasn't. She stretched out her arms and took a deep breath, kissing Andre one last time before drifting off to sleep. Sharing a bed with Andre was worth every wrong that happened to her. It was worth more than the island package itself. It was so magical that Sophia was certain that you couldn't put a price on it. Sophia never wanted this moment to end.

Sophia awoke to a heat burning below her waist. She could feel fingers gently spreading the lips of her pussy with a wet, phallic-shaped object beginning to encircle her clit. She moaned in ecstasy and looked down. Andre pulled his mouth off of her clit and smiled up at her.

"Good morning beautiful," Andre whispered. "I thought I'd thank you for last night."

Sophia just shook her head and smiled. She was still too tired to try to find words. Besides, Andre waking her up with oral sex was too good to interrupt with chitchat.

Andre buried his face back into her snatch knowing that Sophia was content with what he was doing. He continued encircling her clit with his tongue, pressing harder into it with each stroke. He licked the slits of her pussy up and down, teasing her pussy to want even more. He then stuck his tongue into her hole and penetrated it with force. Sophia was practically screaming.

"I can't handle it, Andre," Sophia pleaded. "Get inside me, please!"

Andre didn't need to have her ask him twice. The stiffened cock covered with pre-cum that he was stroking while giving Sophia oral sex was begging to be inside of her. He quickly lifted himself on top of Sophia and placed his dick into her already wet pussy. He shoved it in and out of her gently, indulging in Sophia's moans that followed.

"You can fuck me harder," Sophia stated while teasing Andre's eyes with hers. "I'm not going to break. I promise."

Andre shoved his cock in and out of her hot pussy, feeling its muscles clench. He lifted up the nightshirt he had given her to wear and unleashed the breasts he had been dying to touch. They lay there swollen, big, and beautiful. They had to be at least a D cup, he thought. He pulled at a nipple, making Sophia moan louder than she already was. Watching the other bounce up and down with each stroke of his dick was turning him on. Andre loved big breasts and stuck the nipple that he was rubbing between his fingers into his mouth. He sucked on the erect nipple, licking the sides of it with his tongue. He felt Sophia's pussy clench his cock as she gushed all over him.

Without words, Andre shoved harder into her cunt, feeling his member unleash inside of her. His cum felt so good, the thought of protection never even crossed his mind. If Sophia would get pregnant, he'd make this woman his wife. Hell, if he could have Sophia for the rest of his life he would.

Sophia sat on the edge of the boat while sipping a tall glass of wine. She watched as the water splashed onto the boat, each droplet consuming all of her senses. The water was awakening her from a slumber that she hadn't realized she had been sleeping in. For the first time in years, Sophia felt alive. It was almost as if the essence to her soul had been lost, and Sophia was finally finding its pieces to glue back together again.

Andre walked toward the outline of the beautiful woman sitting still on the edge of his boat. She was true goddess, even her shadow he found gorgeous in the Caribbean sunset. Andre never wanted to let this woman go. Thoughts raced throughout his mind, knowing that Sophia would soon be leaving. She was only a tourist after all; there was no way that she would be staying with him. Andre was certain that he only had a day at the most to keep her by his side. He quickly made plans in his head as he approached her, determined not to allow her to see the sadness in his eyes.

"Hi gorgeous," he said while sitting down next to her and putting his arm around her shoulder. "The sunset is beautiful here, don't you think?"

"Absolutely phenomenal," replied Sophia, resting her head onto Andre's shoulder and looking up into his eyes. "Everything about this place is breath taking, including you."

Andre shot a weak smile at Sophia, sensing the sorrow in her tone. Of all the women he had met in Paris and on Martinique, why was it the woman who didn't live in the same country was the one he was falling so hopelessly in love with? Andre didn't even know much about this woman besides the fact that she was pediatrician and lived in a state called Virginia. Maybe now wasn't the best time for him to ask her more about her life. Maybe now was the time to just enjoy her company, to enjoy each breath they exhaled and inhaled with one another, but Andre couldn't help but to want to find the answers to the questions he was thinking.

"Do you have a lover back home, Sophia?" Andre asked bluntly.

Sophia was taken aback. She hadn't thought about Damien or April. It was almost as if they were disappearing from her memory as each wave splashed onto the boat. She sat still, mindfully considering what she should tell him.

"I'm married," Sophia blurted out.

They sat in silence, Andre choking on the words that were failing to come out of his mouth.

"Married?" he questioned, a mortified look on his face. "Why didn't you tell me?"

"When did I have the time?" asked Sophia who was now out of the grasp of Andre's arms and standing. "We never had time to discuss such matters, Andre. I didn't think it really mattered."

"I guess not," Andre replied dimly. "We've just been two animals acting out on lust. I'd be a fool to think there was anything deeper between us."

What was that supposed to mean? Was Andre falling in love with her? Sophia now leaned against the bars on the side of his boat, looking out into the pale blue water. She hadn't realized until now, but she was starting to fall for the man that now sat grimly beside her. Damien had crossed her mind the night before, but when she awoke to Andre making love to her this morning, she had forgotten about the life that she actually lived. This island was only a vacation; it wasn't real. It was just as good as looking at a photograph and running away with the beauty of life in which it portrayed. This wasn't real; this was just an adventure. Andre hadn't really been hers; neither had been the boat, the blue water, or the crystal clear sky. This island adventure had only been a borrowed moment in time that she now had to give back.

"I have to go," Sophia finally replied after what seemed like days of silence had passed them by.

"Sophia, please don't. Not yet." Andre pleaded. "I just want one more night with you, one more night to feel this passion, our happiness. I never met a woman who made me want more than a good time. I had always been such a busy man. I hadn't had time to invest in something as silly as love and romance. But with you, Sophia, every moment has been worth savoring. Every moment has made me feel so alive. I don't care that you're married, whatever your story may be. I just want to experience our passion one more night. Please, Sophia."

Sophia looked at Andre, her mouth open but failing to fill with air. Did he love her – true, passionate love? She had to admit that in just the last two days they had spent with each other, she felt more for him than she ever did her husband. Why did she feel so responsible for loving Damien, after all that he had done to her? Guilt still weighed heavy in her heart as she determined herself responsible for Damien's affair with April. If only she had been a better wife, he wouldn't have felt so obliged to have sex with another woman. She had known Damien for a long enough time now to know that he was not a cheater. She had watched him as he begged for her affection. She had watched him as she watched herself show him nothing more than the coldness of her heart.

She examined Andre's face, the depression that formed in the creases of his eyebrows. This man was beautiful and she had hurt him. He was the most gorgeous man on the face of the planet as far as she was concerned, yet what they had together was only an affair. She had done unto Damien as what he had done to her. They were even now and she had to go home to face him. She had no other option but to go home. She had to return to her life as the pediatrician and moderately happy housewife. She had to give Damien a chance to make it work. What other choice did she have? She couldn't mold her life into a man's who lived all the way across the sea. What Sophia had lived was a fairytale in which she had finally met her Prince Charming, but now the story was over. She had to close the book and move on.

"I have a husband," Sophia replied firmly. "I have a husband who may have cheated on me, but didn't deserve to be cheated on. He loved me and I refused to love him back. He had reason to do what he did to me; I do not have the reason to follow in his footsteps. I have to go back home, Andre. I have a husband there. I have a family there. I have a life. To stay with you here would only be a mere dream."

"It doesn't have to be a dream, Sophia," started Andre, attempting to persuade her. "I don't know the story behind what you and your husband had shared, but I know what was felt between us. You can't deny that feeling, Sophia. What we have shared has been surreal. I will do anything for you if it means being a part of your life."

Tears were beginning to fall down the sides of Sophia's face.

"My heart doesn't rightfully belong to you, Andre. Please take me back to the island."

The path from the port to the hotel seemed to stretch out in front of Sophia for what seemed like miles. She hesitantly walked up its path, telling herself not to look back. She could feel Andre's eyes on her. It felt as if he was projecting his sadness onto her, but Sophia knew deep down that the sadness she was experiencing was of her own. She was just lying to herself. She had to tell herself that the love that they had shared wasn't hers. Andre deserved a woman who could stay with him, who could love him, and who could cherish him. How would Sophia ever be able to give this to him when she wasn't even able to give it to her husband? She continued walking, never turning her head.

Sophia felt as hollow as the key she was putting into her hotel room's door. She couldn't wait for the door to open, so she could lie on the bed and cry herself to sleep. She spent the last few days pushing aside all of her emotions, not giving chance to look inside for the answers she needed so desperately. The door opened.

"Damien?" Sophia gasped, standing still in the doorframe. "How did you get here? How long have you been here?"

She examined the flowers that were laid on the comforter.

"I got here last night," Damien responded, embracing the fixed Sophia that was now trembling inside. "Where have you been? I was starting to get worried."

Sophia backed away.

"Uh.....with some ladies that I met here at the resort," she responded, lying through her teeth. "Why are you here?"

"Soph..." Damien started. "I know that I fucked up. I know that I don't deserve you after doing what I did. But I never meant to have sex with April; you have to believe me, I swear! I went to her to confide in her. To be honest Soph, you've been so cold to me, so distant. I thought that you were cheating on me. I went to her and asked her about this. I never expected her to come on to me."

Sophia stood still, frozen in time.

"Sophia," continued Damien, as he walked toward her and cupped her face with his hands." All I ever wanted was you. I wanted you to love me. I wanted your affection. I never meant to do this to you. You are my wife and the woman I want to spend the rest of my life with."

Thoughts were now swarming inside of Sophia's mind, but Damien hushed them, kissing her on the lips. Sophia kissed him back passionately, forgetting the moments she had spent with Andre. His lips were sending a tingling sensation down her spine. This was her husband, she was meant to do this with him.

They fell together on the bed, Sophia now grinding on top of him feeling his manhood clenching for life. She licked his lips, smiling at the ecstasy that unleashed underneath his breath. She sat up, the straps of her tank top sexily falling to the sides of her arms. Damien groaned, reaching out with his hands to expose her luscious melons. They sat beautifully over the cloth of the tank top; he took both hands to pinch their nipples. Sophia leaned her head back and moaned, as chills ran throughout her body. She wanted to pleasure the man who was able to bring her such a sensation. She leaned down and slithered to the zipper of his pants, unleashing the alert cock inside. She playfully sucked on its tip and began licking up and down its shaft. Her eyes glanced up in hopes of seeing the look in Andre's face as she pleasured him, but she saw Damien slyly smiling down at her instead. She stopped.

"I don't love you, Damien," she said sharply, as she concealed her tits behind the tank top while sitting up. "I never loved you.

I'm sorry."

"How can you say that, Sophia?" Damien asked, his cock now lying limp before her. "You married me didn't you? The fire just burnt out, Sophia; we can relight it."

"The passion was never there," Sophia responded. "Admit it, Damien, it was never there. When we first started dating, we didn't share many interests. We had great sex, but that was all. I kept telling myself that it would get better and that we could make a relationship and grow into one another. Once two years passed, although I wasn't happy, I decided to marry you. I've always felt like I owed you something, like one day I could make this all up to you. I thought maybe marrying you would give me the motivation to do so, but it didn't. If anything, it made things worse. It just made me constantly feel guilty for not having an emotion that I thought I needed to have. We need to stop lying to one another. I love you as a friend, Damien, I truly do, but you know that we don't belong together. You slept with April because she was your type. You slept with April because you knew that she was the woman who could rock your world. You two have always been compatible. April saw you first; you fell in love with me instead because you were too scared to pursue her."

Damien now looked like a crumbled piece of paper sitting on the bed. He sat silent, taking in Sophia's words and pondering them.

"You are right, Sophia," said Damien, finally interrupting the silence between them. "You are my best friend and I love you for that, but you are right. April was always the woman in back of my mind. You're gorgeous, sexy, and ravishing if I may say so, but it's true that April was always the one I was attracted to, not because she was any more beautiful than you, but because we clicked."

Sophia stood there relieved that they finally had shared truth with one another.

"Go find the man you fell for on this island, Sophia. I've never seen you look happier."

Without responding to Damien, Sophia ran out of the hotel room and down the stairs to the lobby. She flew out of the glass doors of the entrance wondering how Damien knew that she met somebody here on the island. Was he watching her? Or did Damien just have damn good judge of her character? A smile formed on her face knowing for the first time in their relationship that she felt free, not an ounce of guilt traveling through her veins.

She rushed onto the beach, feeling the island's hot sun, while searching the port for Andre's boat. He could've left by now; why on earth would he have stayed yearning for the woman who shattered his heart into a million pieces? She could see the outline of his boat in the distance. He was still there.

She ran as fast as she could, her heart beating so hard inside of her chest that she was sure that it was going to explode any minute now. She needed to see Andre. She had to see Andre, to embrace him with her arms and to kiss his lips with every ounce of passion she had burning inside of her. She was almost at his boathouse when she stopped. The awakening waters that seemed to breathe life into her once frozen body had now turned into an ocean of blackness engulfing each breath she had left. There was Andre on the port, talking to another woman.

Sophia, who was now an android, slowly turned around. How asinine of her to actually think this man loved her. With looks like his, he probably took tourists back to his boathouse all of the time to screw them. Sophia was just one of those tourists. Now she was headed back to the hotel, without Damien and without Andre. At least, Sophia thought, she'd have two supportive friends to go home to. Damien and April would be great together and Sophia would now still have them in her life.

Footsteps were beating across the sand. Sophia, although morose, was feeling angry with the person running behind her. Her emotions were too savage from hurt and deceit; she sure as hell didn't want some dumb kid to kick sand all over her. She turned around to confront them.

"Andre?" she asked in disbelief.

"Sophia!" he yelled, catching his breath and coming to a complete stop in front of her. "Please don't leave."

"I'm not," she responded determined, smiling at the grin on Andre's face.

"Damien came to my hotel," she continued. "He wanted to try to work things out between us. He wanted me to love him again."

"And?" Andre asked, suspense in his eyes.

"And we came to a conclusion," Sophia began. "We both realized that we share love as friends, not lovers. He loves someone else."

"And you?" Andre asked, hoping to help conceal the pain that may have been in her heart.

"I realized that I love you," Sophia replied, leaning into Andre and kissing his lips gently.

"This island awakened me," Sophia continued, stepping back from the kiss and looking into Andre's eyes. "You have awakened me, Andre. You make me feel so alive."

Andre made no eye contact with Sophia as she spoke. He was reaching in his pockets, searching for something. A little black box came out, his hands opening it in front of Sophia, rushing to reveal its contents.

"The woman you saw me talking to at the port was a good friend of mine." Andre started. "A jeweler, in fact. In my heart, I knew that you would come back for me, so I waited."

Andre kept his eyes on Sophia's and leaned down onto one knee.

"Marry me?" he asked.

"Of course I will Andre!" she exclaimed, tears forming in her eyes.

"What is your last name, Andre?"

"Boucher," Andre responded, excitedly.

Sophia smiled. She was going to be Mrs. Andre-Sophia Boucher.

AUTHOR'S NOTE

Readers: I want to expand a few of the stories to see where the characters can be explored further. If there are any of the stories that you would like to read more about again, I'd love to hear from you!

Visit my blog at
http://www.jessicabankman.com

Join my newsletter for free exclusive previews
http://www.jessicabankman.com/in

Follow me on Twitter at
http://www.twitter.com/jessicabankman

Like my page on Facebook at
http://www.facebook.com/jessicabankman

Discover my books at major ebook retailers everywhere